A Less Than Perfect Peace

A Less Than Perfect Peace

Written by

Jacqueline Levering Sullivan

Eerdmans Books for Young Readers
Grand Rapids, Michigan • Cambridge, U.K.

Text © 2014 Jacqueline Levering Sullivan

Published 2014 by Eerdmans Books for Young Readers,
an imprint of Wm. B. Eerdmans Publishing Co.
2140 Oak Industrial Dr. NE, Grand Rapids, Michigan 49505
P.O. Box 163, Cambridge CB3 9PU U.K.

www.eerdmans.com/youngreaders

14 15 16 17 18 19   8 7 6 5 4 3 2 1

Library of Congress Cataloging-in-Publication Data

Sullivan, Jacqueline Levering.
A less than perfect peace / by Jacqueline Levering Sullivan.
pages cm
Sequel to: Annie's war.
Summary: "Fourteen-year-old Annie Howard is determined to help her father
embrace life once again as the Cold War grips the nation. In the midst of her efforts,
she meets and befriends two refugees from Holland, and comes to see the world
differently and understand a bit about the nature of sacrifice" — Provided by publisher.
ISBN 978-0-8028-5431-5
[1. Family life — Washington (State) — Fiction. 2. Refugees — Fiction.
3. Veterans — Fiction. 4. Cold War — Fiction.
5. Washington (State) — History — 20th century — Fiction.]
I. Title.
PZ7.S9518Le 2014
[Fic] — dc23
2013030889

For Peter, Wallace, and Duff.

— *J. L. S.*

Chapter 1

It was the winter of 1950, and folks in Tacoma couldn't stop talking about those evil Russians and wondering if the whole world might just get blown to smithereens. And if that wasn't enough to scare the wits out of a person, the first of January brought the news that the U.S. was planning to build a hydrogen bomb. Sounded to me like the atom bomb was kind of puny in comparison. And what really put everyone on edge was thinking about all those Communist spies and secret agents who might be spreading out all over the place like chicken pox.

But come January 13 — a Friday, wouldn't you know it — a big old blizzard blew in and pretty much knocked everyone off balance. Folks had to stop worrying about the Cold War and start digging out of a real serious cold spell of their own. None of the fellows on the radio could make up their minds. Some said that the storm brought ten inches of snow, but others said it was more like twenty. Didn't matter who was right, there was a ton of it. That nasty old storm produced the coldest recorded temperature in Pierce County since 1916. The wind was so fierce and the snow blew into drifts so high that I expect none of us noticed the sizable storm clouds brewing in our very own house.

Funny how a bunch of snow could make folks lose track of some really important things. Like, despite Daddy's fine words about being "just dandy," he wasn't.

But he was stubborn. Just before we left Seattle, he told Mama to chuck out the newsletter from an army buddy he'd met in the convalescent hospital back East. Some of the blind vets had started a group, and his old friend had urged him to get involved. Daddy said he didn't need any help, didn't have time, and wasn't the least bit interested in what they had to offer. "I already know Braille, I have my fine white cane, and I rarely find myself needing to use either of them," were his exact words. He rarely said a word about the war anymore. He didn't laugh all that much either, or smile a lot, come to think of it.

He did talk about how he liked nothing better than to hear my "sweet voice" read to him from *Life* magazine. One thing I knew for sure, my voice, sweet or not, wasn't enough. Seemed like a lot of feelings had been simmering just under the surface and no one in the family was brave enough to speak them out loud. Then that blizzard roared in.

First thing that crazy morning, Mama started doling out

chores in her best drill sergeant voice. Nothing was going the way she'd planned. She was a bundle of nerves. This was the weekend she had planned to hold the grand opening of her very own beauty salon downtown. When things didn't quite go the way she wanted, Mama had a way of fluttering around the house like a wild bird trapped indoors, bumping into anything or anyone standing in her way.

I figured everyone was jittery. The war had been over for almost five years, and my parents must have wondered when in the world, if ever, our lives would settle down and be the same as before. They'd been hoping a move from Seattle to Tacoma would make our lives about perfect, but — holy cow! — they were probably setting themselves up for a letdown. Nevertheless, we had packed up and moved just after Thanksgiving.

Up until the blizzard, I'd been working like crazy on the school play. I even had a few lines. I'd complained to my Uncle Billy, "Why me, the new girl? Why pick me? You know I'm going to do something dopey, like trip on my dress or forget my lines."

Lucky for me that storm had come along and stopped the whole town dead in its tracks. Step a foot outside that day and you'd get blown inside out like an umbrella. Classes at my junior high and the school play were both canceled.

But Mama didn't let a little bit of icy wind slow her down, not even one straight from the Arctic. She insisted that since my school was closed, I could just come with her to the shop. "There's tons to do, and I'm going to need someone to stock the shelves and sweep and a dozen other things."

There was no use arguing. If I'd said no, Mama would have acted all sniffy, like I'd turned down an offer to help the starving children in Europe.

"I don't trust Billy to get us downtown in that battered old pickup of his. We'll take the bus," she said.

We put on extra sweaters and our heavy wool coats. We wrapped ourselves in scarves and pulled on warm hats. I put on two pairs of itchy gloves. We waddled to the front door and opened it to a wall of white. The drifts were piled smack against the house. Not a sign of the porch swing.

Mama didn't even blink. "We'll just go out the back," she said. "We can walk down the alley to the bus stop."

But when we opened the back door, the yard and the alley had pretty much disappeared under a thick blanket of snow. Not a problem for Mama. She had set her mind on getting to that shop. "It's opening day," she hollered into the wind. Like maybe if she shouted those words out into the storm, it would just settle down.

When we walked back into the kitchen, Daddy was at the stove pouring a cup of coffee. I watched him place his thumb on the top edge of the cup so he could tell when it was nearly full. He'd learned a few things at the hospital in Connecticut, like tuning in to echoes to help him get a sense of his surroundings, but he'd also come up with a few tricks of his own. He followed the clothesline when he went out to the workshop next to the garage. He imagined his dinner plate was a clock and we'd say, "Meat loaf at six o'clock and mashed potatoes at three-fifteen." We never talked much about him being blind.

"Daddy, the snow is piled up so high outside, we can't see the garage door. Billy will have to shovel his way up to the back porch." Uncle Billy had a little apartment over the garage.

"That wind sounds mean," said Daddy. "I've been listening to the radio. We're in for a bad storm, no doubt about it." He took a sip of his coffee and sat down at the kitchen table. "Annie Leigh, come sit down," he said and patted the chair next to his. "I'd be real surprised if you're going anywhere this morning."

I hung up my coat in the back hall and stuffed my wool hat and gloves into the pockets. "Mama's determined to go downtown. She's out in the hall calling a taxi," I said and slipped into the chair next to Daddy.

"No taxi's going to come out here in this weather. I bet you a dollar no buses are running either." Daddy got up to top off his coffee. I didn't offer to help. Daddy could get real prickly when folks tried to lend a hand.

He could make out bright colors and a few shapes, so the first thing we bought after he returned from the war was a set of dishes all the colors of the rainbow. I expect just knowing the red sugar bowl from the blue cups helped Daddy feel a little more independent.

"You know Mama," I said, watching him make his way back to the table. "Once she's made up her mind she's going to do something, even General MacArthur couldn't stop her."

"Like that darn shop," said Daddy. "I don't know why she has to have her own beauty salon. As soon as Billy and I get our new carpentry business up and running, she won't have to work. There'll be plenty to do right here."

Daddy had always believed one day he'd have his own carpentry business. It was his dream. I didn't say anything, but I knew Mama. She was on a mission. Opening up her own beauty shop was just as important to her. Grandma Hattie knew just how important and had loaned her the money to get started. Mama and Daddy were both stubborn as mules.

The kitchen door flew open with a whack. "Can you believe it, Eddie? No taxicabs. Not one." Mama gave a big sigh and looked frantically around the kitchen, like maybe she'd find the answer to her problem on the wall or in the cupboards. For a minute I had a vision of the two of us sledding our way downtown in the dishpan. I choked back a giggle. Mama, on the other hand, was dead serious. "I bet we could go along the Hinkles' fence and find our way to the bus stop."

Daddy just sat there shaking his head. He knew she'd already made up her mind. Just about the time he was ready to give her a million reasons why going to the shop was a dumb idea, we heard Uncle Billy run up the back steps and stop long enough to stomp the snow off his shoes before bursting into the kitchen. He leaned over the sink and shook snow from his hair. "Dang! Now this here is a real doggone blizzard!"

Mama took a quick sip of Daddy's coffee and started to button up her coat. "Blizzard! You're such a kidder, Billy. Tacoma doesn't have blizzards. This is just a pesky old snow flurry."

Billy gave me a wink and rolled his eyes for emphasis. I made a face and let out a groan.

Mama didn't miss a beat. She went out into the hall and came back with my coat. "C'mon, Annie, we're going down to the shop."

"Geez Louise! It must be freezing out there!"

"Now don't whine, Annie. I need you today." Mama put on her old felt hat and dug around in her pocket book for her gloves.

Daddy cleared his throat. "Dorothy, unless you're a polar bear, I don't think it's safe to go traipsing around out there. I can still hear that wind; in fact, I can feel it rattle the house every so often. This is no weather to be standing around waiting for a bus knee-deep in snow."

I looked at Mama. She wasn't going to budge. No one ever called her anything but her nickname, Dory. "Dorothy" was saved for serious conversations. I always paid attention to

Daddy when he talked about what he heard. He could figure out lots of things from just listening. For sure, he was right about the storm.

I turned to Uncle Billy for help. He shook his head and threw up his hands. "Don't look at me, kiddo." He lowered his voice to a whisper. "I'm not gettin' into the middle of this. One thing I'll tell you — put on high-top galoshes over your shoes. That wet will seep right through and freeze your toes."

Daddy stood up and reached out for Mama's arm. She leaned in closer, and he muttered something into her ear. Her face turned tomato red.

"We'll be fine," she snapped back. "Annie Leigh, put on your coat. We're going." Mama turned on her heel and went to the back hall and came back with a ratty old pair of rain boots. "We'll take the bus both ways," she said and sat down to wrestle her shoes into the boots.

"You bet," said Billy. "I'm not going anywhere in this mess. I'm going to make Eddie and me a big stack of buttermilk pancakes, and maybe, just maybe, later I'll plow through that walk out there and see if I can get that blasted heater going in the workshop." He disappeared into the pantry, where I knew he'd stay until we left.

I struggled into a pair of old galoshes — they never fit right over my saddle shoes — then wrapped myself up again and tromped out the back door and into three-foot drifts. I had half a mind to just dash back into the house, no matter the consequences.

But Mama grabbed my hand and dragged me along in the space between our garage and Mrs. Hinkle's side fence. I could hardly walk for all the deep pockets of snow. "Mama, do you know where you're going? I can barely see. We're going to get lost." Even though she was right in front of me, I wasn't sure she could hear me. The wind was fierce.

"Nonsense," she yelled over her shoulder. "We're almost to the alley." She gave my hand a yank. "Then we just have to follow the Hinkles' back fence to the end of the street, and we'll have a short walk to the bus stop."

Our short walk seemed to take forever. The wind bit my face and crept straight into my clothes, sending chills clear through to my bones. Mama stomped a path for me, but I was still knee-deep in snow the whole way. By the time we reached the bus stop, it hurt to breathe, and I could only gasp.

"See," she said, "w-we made it." She was shivering so hard her words came out like little screams. The corner was deserted. No buses in sight. No cars. A mound of white covered the bus bench like a giant puffy quilt.

"We need to go back. No bus is going to show up, and it's starting to snow harder. I can't feel my face." I tugged at her sleeve. "We're going to freeze solid, stiff as two ironing boards. Our bodies won't be found until the thaw."

"C'mon, don't be a crybaby; we're tough." Mama's voice was tight from the cold. "Let's sing something. Keep our minds off the weather."

Of course, that didn't happen. Our breath froze in our chests before we could get out the first notes. We stomped circles around the bus bench, trying to get warm.

"This is crazy. I'm going to start home. My toes have turned into icicles." I was not going to freeze and die a martyr's death waiting for a smelly bus belching exhaust.

"Just give it a few more minutes. I can't believe the bus company shuts down for a little snow." Mama was trying to sound hopeful, but her teeth were chattering. "And don't you dare start off on your own."

"Just look at the streets. Do you see any buses coming?" I could barely see a foot in front of me and had no idea which direction would take us home.

"All right, all right. We'll go home." Mama reached for my hand. "We'll have to walk into the wind, so don't let go."

We had nothing to follow. The flurries of snow had covered our tracks, but we walked for quite a while and still no Hinkles' fence. In fact, I could swear we were going in circles. When I saw the outlines of the little market across from the bus stop, I knew we'd gone nowhere at all.

I let go of Mama's hand. "We aren't getting anywhere." I pointed across the street. "Isn't that Wolfe's Market?"

"Now how could that be?"

I figured it was a cruel joke to be lost a block and a half from home. "We need to go back the other way," I yelled and turned us around and headed in what I hoped was the direction home.

We went in zigzag circles for a good long while before Uncle Billy showed up in his frayed old army coat looking like Sasquatch on snowshoes and led us back home, Mama protesting the whole way.

Chapter 2

We stumbled into the warm kitchen throwing off snow like wet dogs. Daddy was waiting for us with a pot of hot tea and deep worry lines etched into his forehead.

"Thank God!" He tried to sound stern, but I heard that sharp crack in his voice. He'd been worried sick. Daddy reached over and patted my shoulder, feeling for my sleeve. "I couldn't hear a single car moving, so I was sure the streets hadn't been plowed and you two were stranded out in the cold somewhere frozen to the bone. You need to get out of those damp clothes. You'll catch pneumonia standing around in wet wool."

I let Daddy help me out of my coat. Mama had already thrown hers over one of the hooks by the back door and was bustling around the kitchen rattling the dishes, but she didn't say a word. I waited for the room to go all quiet, the way it does when Daddy and Mama are heading for one of their "airing of views" discussions. I waited to hear that tone in her voice, watching for that upward tilt to her nose, when she makes it clear she knows better than anyone what is best.

Uncle Billy jumped in before either one could say a harsh word. "We never expected you to last as long as you did." He swallowed a snort and poked two more pieces of wood into the stove to build up the fire. "I tell you, Eddie," he said, fanning his hands over the stove for warmth, "that storm is something else. I'm going to bring in some more wood from the garage. Looks like we'll be snowbound over the weekend."

When he stepped out the door, the wind practically blew Billy off the porch and into the snow. Mama was right behind him, ready to make sure the back door was shut tight.

She couldn't seem to stand still. I expected to see a hole worn in the kitchen linoleum by dinner. She was a mess of fidgets. Mama always expected things to fall into place just the way she'd planned. "I can't imagine what Emmie and Gilly will think if no one shows up at the shop. I'd better go give them a call." Mama scurried off to the phone in the front hall.

She'd hired Emmie Todd and Gilly Pearce right out of beauty school. They were both pretty as a picture. Emmie could name all the colors in Revlon nail polish — "Cherries in the Snow" was my favorite — and Gilly knew all about the new permanent waves. Dorothy's House of Beauty was going to be up on all the new hairstyles. Mama had also ordered a bunch of magazines for the shop like *The Saturday Evening Post* and *Vogue* and my favorite, *Life*. She'd also decided that fresh flowers from the new florist on the first floor would make the salon look extra special.

Mama's excitement did not carry much weight with Daddy. He'd stayed real quiet while Billy was out getting wood and Mama was on the phone. He just felt his way around the kitchen, picking up the breakfast dishes and stacking them in the dishpan to wash. I went to the pantry and got a dishtowel from the pile neatly stacked next to Mama's recipe box.

"I'll wash if you dry, Daddy," I said, and landed a big sloppy kiss on his cheek.

He took the towel and mumbled something under his breath, but I ignored it. Daddy was happier when he had things to do. Kept him from getting all out of sorts. He got real grouchy if he sat around all day.

Before the war took his sight, Daddy could build just about anything, from a dining room table to a chest of drawers. Even now he could wax and polish wood to a shine you could see yourself in, and choose a perfect piece of wood just by feel or smell. For most things, though, he needed a little help. I was pretty sure he missed his old life something fierce.

"So, my girl," he said, "you disappointed about missing your stage debut?" He stood next to me at the sink and carefully stacked the plates as he dried, measuring the space with his fingers to keep the dishes from sliding off.

"Not really. To tell you the truth I just got the part because some girl got mumps. It was more fun being on the stage crew helping paint the sets. I even got to do one whole backdrop, a bunch of old trees with branches like witches' arms. I made them really spooky." I rinsed the last dish and put it in the rack. Daddy patted my arm with a damp hand. "That's swell, honey. Your grandma was telling me she thought you had a real knack for drawing."

Something was on his mind. He wiped at the plate for the longest time before hanging the towel next to the stove to dry. "Once Billy and I are making some real money, I'm going to get your mama a new electric range and get rid of this old iron monster." Daddy gave a half-hearted kick in the direction of the stove. "It eats up a ton of wood, and it's a fire hazard." He let out a big sigh and sat down so hard, his old armchair re-leased a big poof of dust. "A man has to take care of his family, and I plan to do just that. You bet."

Daddy talked an awful lot about being the man of the house. His blindness had cost him more than just his sight. His corny jokes and silly pranks no longer filled the house with laughter. Of course, just by coming home from the war and be-ing close to me, always ready to listen or give me a hug, Daddy was taking care of me just fine. I wanted to find the right words to let him know that, but before I could get them straight in my head, Billy burst back into the kitchen, carrying a canvas bag full of wood.

"Dang bust it! A fella could fall into a drift and get lost on his way to the back steps."

Billy and I were still stacking firewood in the box when Mama came back.

"Well, I got through to both girls. Seems none of the streets have been cleared. I suppose if they can't make it, our customers can't either." Mama bustled around the kitchen, lining up the canisters and restacking the dried dishes before she put them away. "Guess I'll just make us a fresh pot of coffee, and maybe Annie will stir us up a batch of molasses cookies."

And so we all just stayed in the warm kitchen, the soap operas playing in the background. Dopey *Ma Perkins* and that other silly one, *Stella Dallas*, Mama's favorites. Uncle Billy and I couldn't resist imitating Ma Perkins and her friend Shuffle for Daddy's benefit and teasing Mama when she began to tear up over Stella's wretched life.

After I took them out of the oven, my molasses cookies barely had time to cool before they disappeared. Uncle Billy read Daddy a bunch of articles out of the *Tribune*. Mama kept remembering folks to call and would run out into the cold hall, only to rush back minutes later and warm herself at the stove. I took out the last pan of cookies and then went to look for some drawing paper and a carpenter's pencil. It was going to be a long afternoon. Uncle Billy made one more trip out for wood and declared it was his last until the next morning when he said they absolutely had to start on their workshop, freezing weather or not.

By five-fifteen, when it was time for *Portia Faces Life*, I couldn't face Portia or another molasses cookie. Uncle Billy was asleep by the stove, sitting up in Daddy's chair, snoring in little short bursts like a freight train. Mama and Daddy were across from each other at the kitchen table, talking in hushed voices. Our happy little family. A thought I didn't hold too long. Mama suddenly pulled her hand away, stood up, and stormed out into the cold back hall. A sudden shiver slid down my spine, right there in our warm, toasty, molasses-smelling kitchen.

Chapter 3

It would be almost a month before the weather settled into our regular old rain, but only after what Daddy called a "silver thaw." Pipes burst and then the weather warmed up a bit, but the temperature dropped again, and everything was covered in a solid coating of ice.

Things remained pretty icy inside the Howard house as well. Having to put off the opening of the shop for a whole week hadn't helped Mama's mood one bit. That cold patch in her heart hadn't melted even a little. She and Daddy were talking, but their words were definitely frosty. Crammed together in our new house for days on end, and with all the dithering about the new beauty shop, I guess Mama and Daddy had let a lot of old hurts and sorrows fester, and now they were coming to the surface.

Not only did the shop opening have to be canceled, but Daddy and Uncle Billy were frozen out of the workshop, delaying the opening of Howard Brothers Fine Carpentry. Everyone was as cranky as a bunch of prickly porcupines. All kinds of plans were in the works one minute, and all three of them were about to come to blows the next. Eventually, Daddy and Uncle Billy made ponchos out of old army blankets and ended up rattling around in the workshop out back until their fingers nearly froze.

"Dory," Daddy said one morning, after Mama had burned the oatmeal for the second time, "you're going to make your-self sick or drive the rest of us batty if you don't sort out what's bothering you." He made her a cup of tea with honey, but she only waved him off with a little sniff, like maybe the smell of all that burning oatmeal had stuffed up her nose. I grabbed a piece of toast and made a fast retreat to my bedroom. Honestly!

Uncle Billy tried his best to keep Mama from getting Daddy all upset. Every chance he got he'd tease her about the little hiccup sounds she made when she got really uppity. One morning when she started ordering us around, he made a hel-met out of the Sunday paper and goose-stepped all around the kitchen. Mama was not amused. She just let out a string of big sighs and flapped her hands at him. "Billy Howard, you're not one bit funny."

And then she marched off into her "music room," actually the entrance hall near the front door, and pounded out "Don't Fence Me In" on our old upright piano. I was about to lose my patience with everybody.

Late one afternoon I went out to the workshop to help Uncle Billy while he finished hanging shelves. He was still the best person I knew to hear me out about Daddy. I'd never forgotten how my uncle had come back from the war, all torn up inside and the meanest thing on two feet. But after he got into some trouble and Grandma Hattie and I gave him a good talking to, and Daddy returned from the war, Billy began to let go of the terrors he'd bottled up inside. The Uncle Billy itching for a fight had gradually turned into the one who took care of all of us, always willing to drop everything to give a person a hand.

"Do you think Daddy's really doing OK?" I handed Billy the level and waited. He usually had to roll questions around in that noggin of his before he could offer a serious answer.

Billy studied the shelf he was working on. "You know it's been tough for your dad. It's hard for a fellow to sit around a lot of the time, knowing his wife is supporting the family. He needs to feel like the man of the house. Once we start getting customers, he won't have time to feel sorry for himself."

"Once that happens, what's Daddy going to do exactly? He needs important work to do. He'll get tired of busy work real fast."

Billy put down his hammer, and his face tightened into a frown. "Now, Annie, your dad can do a lot of things. And he's got all kinds of ideas. When I get stuck, he's the one who'll know the answer."

"But that's not real work."

"OK. For starters, he can take orders and talk to customers. No one knows wood like your daddy. And he can place orders for supplies and stuff." Billy shook his head and began to concentrate on the next board that needed to be measured. He was quiet for a while before he said any more. "Now don't go mentioning any of this to your dad or your mama — especially not to her. He's doing just fine."

"Doesn't seem to me things are fine or that everything's going to be peachy keen anytime soon." Honestly, I thought Billy would have more sense than to act like everything was just swell. "You, most of all, should have some idea of what Daddy's going through."

"Don't worry your head about that kind of stuff. You leave all that to the adults in this family." Billy gave a row of nails several good whacks. "Seems to me your dad can work out what he wants to do with his life on his own."

I swallowed the lump in my throat and grabbed the broom to sweep up some of the sawdust and the wood curls. But I wasn't finished. "Has Daddy ever mentioned calling that old hospital buddy of his or maybe even getting a guide dog?"

Billy looked at me like I'd lost my mind. "A dog! Your mama hates dogs. She'd have a real fit."

"Not if a dog helped Daddy. Mama would just have to get

used to it. I think we should work on Daddy, try to make him see all the ways he could be more independent."

Billy picked up a new board and started whistling, his signal our conversation was over. Well, I could be pigheaded, too. I hung up the broom, took off my shop apron, and walked off without a word. If he had a mind to, Billy could still make me feel like a little kid again. One of these days I'd fix it so someone in this family had to take me seriously about Daddy. Maybe I could convince him to try and get out on his own sometimes and not have to wait on one of us. Maybe four and a half years wasn't enough time to get the war out of his head. He certainly didn't seem any happier.

After my conversation with Billy, thinking about Daddy kept me awake that night long after the house was quiet. The next day at school I could hardly keep my eyes open. I kept falling asleep in algebra. When I walked into art class, I thought I'd stumbled into the wrong classroom. Instead of our regular teacher, the principal was there. He called us to attention and introduced Miss Lydia Moore. She could have passed for a ninth grader; her hair hung in one long golden braid down her back, and she seemed to float around the classroom like a ballerina. I could picture her in a snow globe, a dancing princess. I couldn't believe she was our new art teacher. The principal mumbled something about "leaving us in capable hands" and made a quick exit.

"I want to get to know all of you as soon as possible," Miss Moore said. "So let's go around and each of you can tell me something about yourself."

Stupid Johnny Ross let out a low whistle and slumped in his seat in a mock faint. The rest of us were struck dumb, and we all stammered through our introductions. I could hardly wait to write Grandma Hattie about a certain Miss Moore, who moved around the classroom like Vera Ellen dancing with Gene Kelly in *On the Town* — the one movie we actually sat through twice.

Miss Moore stayed in my head until social studies, where everyone could talk of nothing else but the rumor that our regular art teacher had been fired after she was seen smoking in the Mayfair Hotel bar. I tried to picture mousy Miss Parker with a martini in one hand and a cigarette in the other. All I could see were her big brown eyes and her baggy brown sweaters.

My mind was so full of gossip it was hard to concentrate on Mr. Raymond's pop quiz. Answering questions about ancient Mesopotamia couldn't hold a candle to passing notes about poor Miss Parker, and I'd just passed a third note under my desk to the girl in front of me when I looked up to see a tall, blond boy standing in the doorway. He wore an awfully confident smile for someone wearing wide, dark pants that flared out around his ankles.

The low murmur of voices brought a sharp "Be quiet" from Mr. Raymond, who had retreated to his usual chair in the back of the room with a Mars bar and a Zane Grey novel.

When our voices only became louder, he hopped up and scurried to the front of the room, brushing at bits of chocolate on his tie. "What is it, young man?" he snapped. "You've interrupted a test."

A chapter of Zane Grey was more like it. The boy handed him a note, and Mr. Raymond practically beamed with delight. "Attention, class! Please welcome Johannes VanderVelde, who comes to us from the Netherlands."

Mr. Raymond glanced around the room. "There, next to Annie Howard." He paused. "Yes, that will do. Annie, raise your hand so Johannes can find you."

I shifted in my seat and gave a little wave. Johannes walked unhurriedly down the row of desks. Even in those silly pants, he knew how handsome he was.

"This seat? No student sits here?" he asked, pointing to the one directly across from mine.

I looked up and felt myself blush. The bluest pair of eyes stared back at me.

"Miss . . . I sit down, yes?"

"No — that is, yes. I mean, no. I mean . . ." I sounded like a babbling idiot. "It's not taken. Yes, you can sit down."

I knew my mouth was stuck open, but I couldn't seem to

close it. Those blue eyes danced. He was laughing at me.

"Now, Johannes," Mr. Raymond began. "Tell us something about yourself."

And for the rest of class, the test forgotten, Johannes VanderVelde was the center of attention. We never did settle down. Turned out Johannes was a Dutch refugee. He and his twin sister had come to Tacoma to live with an aunt and uncle. I wondered where his folks were, but I didn't ask. Everyone was talking at once, and we didn't pay any attention when the class bell rang. Mr. Raymond dashed around grabbing our neglected tests before shooing us out the door. I was halfway to home ec when Johannes tapped me on the shoulder.

"Please, could you tell me where I find this shop?" He looked genuinely puzzled and held out his schedule.

I tried to look at it, but my attention was drawn to an angry red scar on his wrist that wound snake-like around his lower arm and disappeared under his shirt sleeve.

"Oh," I said, "you mean wood shop. I have a class right across the hall. I'll show you."

We pushed our way down the crowded corridor together. "This is it, Johannes," I said when we'd reached the shop class-room. "Right through this door."

He surprised me by taking my hand. "You call me Jon, OK? How do I call you?"

"Annie," I answered in a half whisper. A giant bullfrog had

jammed in my throat. And I absolutely refused to believe those blue eyes had anything to do with my heart beating so hard against my ribs that I was certain they would break.

"We are friends, yes?" His eyes danced again. As the door closed behind him, Johannes turned and smiled. I smiled back. My feet couldn't seem to budge, so I stood in the middle of the hall for a second studying my shoes. When I finally looked up, Johannes was still there, those blue eyes peering at me through the little square window at the top of the door.

Chapter 4

On the way home from school my head was so full of Johannes I daydreamed a half-block out of my way before I realized it. I couldn't wait to tell Daddy about Miss Moore and Miss Parker, but I wasn't going to say a word about Johannes. What I really wanted was to shout, "Hey, everybody. I met this new boy today at school. He's from Holland, and he's got the bluest eyes and the dreamiest smile I've ever seen." But that would sound just plain dumb, and I'd never hear the end of it.

As it turned out, I didn't get to tell anybody anything, at least not that afternoon. Daddy was sitting in the living room by himself with all the shades down. He didn't even answer when I called hello from the front hall. Mama was still in her grey tweed coat and hat sulking in the kitchen. The house smelled of gardenias. Three floated in a bowl on the kitchen table and Mama was wearing one on her lapel. The sickening sweet smell always made me want to puke. Besides, if you touched them, they got all brown and icky. But Mama loved them.

"You're home early," I said. "Why's Daddy all by himself in the living room?"

"Honestly, he's getting impossible. All I did was get a ride home. The one time we had all the hair dryers going in the shop, would you believe it, we blew the electricity in the entire building. Had to shut down the shop." Mama drummed her fingers on the table.

"Daddy's sitting out there looking grumpy. Does it have anything to do with these?" I poked at the gardenia in the center of the table.

"I told your dad that everyone got flowers. Larry — Mr. Capaldi, the florist in the shop below — gave us all flowers." Mama stood up, carefully unpinning her gardenia and setting it gently into the bowl with the others. "I don't know what's gotten into your dad. It was nice not to have to ride that old rattle-trap bus for a change." Mama took off her coat and threw it over the back of a chair. "Besides, with the electricity off, the shop gardenias were going to wilt anyway. And who doesn't like flowers once in a while?"

Every chance I got I pinched those ugly flowers until Mama had no choice but to throw them out. I couldn't be certain, but it seemed to me Daddy's mood improved considerably once that putrid smell no longer filled every room. He never had much of a chance to surprise Mama with flowers. He rarely left the house, so I did most of his shopping for him. I tried to buy things she'd like, but I'm sure it wasn't the same.

The next Saturday we all slept late. Mama had to tickle me awake. No wind to shake the rafters and only the tiniest bit of drizzle. "Get up, lazybones," she said. "You're coming downtown with me today."

I just had time for a few spoonfuls of oatmeal before Mama had us out the door. We'd barely gotten to the bus stop when a florist van pulled up. The driver rolled down the passenger window and yelled at Mama, "Come on, Dorothy, hop in."

He had to be Gardenia Man. The last thing I wanted was to drive downtown with "Larry," but I had to admit I was curious. Mama got in front, and Mr. Capaldi motioned me to a little jump seat in the back.

"Sorry about that," he said. "Hope you don't mind sitting with the flowers."

Mama introduced us, but it was clear that Mr. Larry Capaldi had eyes only for Mama. He was definitely flirting, and Mama was all giggly. Disgusting! What a jerk! I thought I was going to gag.

"Where did all these flowers come from?" I said. "Do you take them home at night or something?"

"Pretty funny, kid." Larry looked at the rearview mirror and smiled at me. "These are flowers for a funeral. They aren't fresh enough for table bouquets, but they work out real well for funeral wreaths."

So in addition to being a jerk, Mr. Larry Capaldi was also a pretty sorry excuse for a florist. At least Mama had stopped giggling. He dropped us right at the front door of the building, and before we got out, he handed Mama a rose. He reached back and carefully picked a carnation out of a big bucket for me. "For you," he said and gave me a little wink. Ugh!

I struggled out of the back of the van and ran up the stairs to the second floor and waited for Mama to come unlock the door. Once inside, I shredded the carnation into the nearest wastebasket while Mama was in the back room.

By the time I'd swept up at least two pounds of hair and unpacked tons of supplies, lunchtime had rolled around. I was determined to get Mama to go to Woolworth's for a sandwich — by ourselves — and then we could go in the back where the piano was and buy the latest sheet music. Whenever we had the time and Maggie the piano lady was there, she would play our favorites for us, and sometimes when we were feeling frisky, Mama and I jitterbugged right there in the back of the store. Maggie never complained if we didn't buy any music. She'd just look at us through her big, sparkly cat-eye glasses and smile. "You gals sure know how to have fun." And then she'd pound out one last tune.

At the lunch counter, we ordered our usual tuna

sandwiches and cherry Cokes, but Mama spoiled everything by talking nonstop about Larry. "He's nice. And funny, too, don't you think?"

"Not particularly." I studied Mama's face. What had gotten into her? She quickly grabbed her purse and paid the bill. Her good mood had definitely turned sour.

"Let's go get the new Jo Stafford song," I said. "You can play it for Daddy when we get home. And, by the way, after work, I don't plan on riding in the back of that cootie-covered florist van. I'm taking the bus."

I was certain Mr. Capaldi had to go miles out of his way to give us a ride. We lived in the old part of town where our neighbors had names like Petrich and Zukowski, hardworking folks, mostly fishermen. Bet Larry never worked all that hard. For sure, he lived somewhere a bit more grand.

Billy's green pickup was there at the curb when we came down the stairs after the last customer. Since it was raining buckets, I had two good reasons for being glad to see him. Mama gave a quick look over her shoulder before we squeezed into the front seat. I tried real hard not to snicker when I saw the lights in the florist were already out.

"Thought I'd better come get you two before you had to swim home." Uncle Billy thumped my knee working the gear shift. "You got a phone call today, Annie Leigh. From your art teacher."

Ever since we moved to Tacoma, I'd been real clear: Annie Leigh was a kid's name. Now it was just plain Annie. Mama and Daddy never remembered, but I figured my uncle would understand. Using my whole name seemed babyish. Next year I'd be in high school, and I didn't want a kid name to follow me. Billy was just being a pest.

Mama was probably thinking about gardenias, so she wasn't really paying much attention to our conversation.

"That Miss Moore had a real nice voice," said Billy. He had a big silly grin on his face. "What's she like?"

Oh, Lord, what was it with us Howards? Practically the whole family was hell-bent on romance. If my uncle horned in, it would take all the fun out of talking about Miss Moore.

"Oh really? I wonder what in the world she could possibly want." I hoped Uncle Billy would butt out if he thought I wasn't the least bit interested.

"Just so happens I know exactly why she called. Seems Parents' Night is coming up, and since she's new, she's calling all her students to urge them to bring their families. I decided I'd do my duty as your uncle and make sure I'm there."

"Geez!" Before I could give him a bad time, Uncle Billy bump-bumped the pickup into the alley behind our house and came to a halt just inches away from the garage. At that point I was seriously considering running away from home.

Even before I reached the back door, I could hear Daddy

whistling. It was a sure sign he was in a much better mood. He'd even put the potatoes on and set the table after a fashion. I could swear I saw his nose wiggle, trying to sniff out any suspect bouquets. I said a little prayer of thanks that we had missed out on any gift flowers, although before we left the shop, Mama had laid on her new Shalimar perfume a bit thick.

Daddy gave me a big hug and a kiss. "How's my girl? I've been waiting all afternoon for you to come home." He patted the sofa cushion next to him. "Come sit a while and talk to me."

If we'd been alone, it might have been a good time to tell him about Johannes. But first I wanted to keep that smile on his face and hear him laugh. Later I'd read him "Hazel" and "Steve Canyon" from the funny pages and tell him about the blue-haired ladies at the shop who still offered me gum and patted my head like I was four. Then we'd throw the curls from the shop out for the birds to warm their nests and maybe we'd listen to *Fibber McGee and Molly* on the radio. Mama had already shut herself up in the bedroom, most likely having one of her sulks.

When Daddy was missing in the war, I wanted nothing more than for him to come home and wrap me up in a big bear hug. Once he was safely back home, what could ever go wrong again? The worst would be over. Trouble was I hadn't counted on him being hurt and needing us to take care of him. Uncle

Billy's war wounds were the kind we couldn't see, and they took a good while to heal. I reached for Daddy's hand and held it tight. One thing I'd learned for sure. A war didn't necessarily end when the fighting stopped.

Chapter 5

Turned out Uncle Billy got his wish and ended up at Parents' Night officially. He was the only Howard available. Daddy had a bad cold, so he stayed at home. Thursday night was Mama's late night at the shop. My uncle was like a little kid when I agreed he could take me. You'd think we were going to the circus.

That night after dinner, when he came back into the kitchen from his apartment, I had to hold down a laugh. His hair was all slicked back in little spit waves, and he had on a clean white shirt and a tie, but his old corduroy jacket was a little ragged around the cuffs. I carefully picked off the piece of tissue stuck to a nick on his chin.

"You have to promise not to get all flirty with Miss Moore," I said. "I mean it, Billy. You'd better not embarrass me."

He just got this big old grin on his face that stayed put most of the evening. And on the way over he asked me all kinds of dumb questions about Miss Moore, like what color her eyes were. Jeepers! What a goof!

Once we got to the junior high, he raced me through my classrooms, barely stopping long enough to meet my teachers. I wanted to stay a while in home ec, secretly hoping Johannes might show up across the hall. Not even homemade fudge was enough to make Billy linger.

"You're just being downright rude," I said. "We've all worked hard on our projects. You could at least pretend to be interested in my education."

"I'm interested. I'm interested, really." Uncle Billy leaned over and whispered into my ear. "When did you get to be such a sorehead?"

I gave him a good punch in the shoulder. "Honestly, Billy!" Before I had a chance to tease my uncle any more, I felt someone behind me. I turned. It was Johannes with a girl as tall as he was, with the same piercing blue eyes. Her hair was braided like a golden crown across her head. She had the rosiest cheeks and was so pretty my heart dropped to my shoes.

"Elisabeth," said Johannes. "My friend Annie."

"Annie, I meet you gladly." Elisabeth let out a giggle. "No, I mean I'm glad to meet you." She clasped her hands together and did a little skip. "You are the girl so kind to Jon, yes?"

Of course, she was his sister. His twin.

Uncle Billy took my elbow. He was eager to steer me down

to art class so he could get all drooly over Miss Moore. I felt my cheeks flush. "Johannes, Elisabeth — this is my uncle."

"Hi kids, nice to meet you." He had no time for small talk. I had to dig in my heels just to say goodbye.

"Will you still be here for . . . " Elisabeth stopped and looked at her brother. He whispered something to her. "Yes, we hope you will stay for refreshments. Our Tante Dee sent over some special cakes. We hope you will get to taste them."

I had just enough time to nod a quick yes before Uncle Billy marched me off down the hall. He suddenly stopped in front of the trophy cabinet to pat down those pesky waves and straighten his tie. "Honest to Pete! Mr. Casanova." He was really getting on my nerves.

He needn't have bothered checking his hair or his tie. Just as we got to the classroom, Mama showed up. She looked like she was dressed for a party, in a tight suit I swear I'd never seen before. Her hair was swept into a big do, and her lipstick was sitting a smidge above her upper lip and a brighter red than usual. Swell! Just swell!

"What are you doing here, Mama? I thought you had to work late." I wasn't at all pleased to see her, and something about her seemed definitely off.

Uncle Billy took in a breath and said, "Wow, Dory! You fall in a barrel of gin?" He looked around, like he expected maybe Daddy would suddenly appear. I noticed he gave a quick glance down the hall. "How'd you get here?" He gave me this look that said, "Now what?" Clearly, our evening wasn't going at all the way we'd planned. "I hear they have refreshments. How about you and Annie getting some coffee?"

"I don't want her anywhere near the cafeteria," I hissed. "What if she makes a scene?"

"Well, we can't take her home like this. What do you suggest?" Uncle Billy grabbed Mama's shoulders in a one-armed hug to keep her steady.

"Take her into that empty classroom across the hall, and I'll go get some coffee. And don't turn the light on." This was the absolute limit. And I'd worried he was the one who was bound to embarrass me.

Mama had a case of the hiccups that wouldn't stop, but once we got her into the classroom and the nearest desk, she started making little gagging sounds. My uncle got a real funny cockeyed look on his face. "On second thought," he said, "you'd better stay with her, in case . . . you know, she needs the little girls' room or something."

"Honestly, Billy. I mean, criminy!" He was right, of course. "OK, but come right back."

I was going to have to play mother. And I had a good mind to tell Mama just what I thought about how she'd been acting. But her head dropped down on the desktop, and she fell right to sleep. She even started to snore. We were just steps away from Miss Moore's classroom. I hoped we wouldn't be discovered before we got Mama back together.

Uncle Billy returned with two cups of coffee and four big ginger snaps sticking out of his jacket pocket. "C'mon, Dory," he said, elbowing her shoulder. "Just what the doctor ordered."

Mama raised her head halfway up and looked around. "What's going on?" She sat up straight for a second and then slumped back into the desk. "Where are we?"

"Here, drink this." I put one of the coffees down in front of her. "And then we'll take you home."

Mama studied the coffee a while before she picked it up and began to take a few tiny sips. Uncle Billy started in on the ginger snaps. He offered me one, complete with pocket lint. I turned him down. It was going to be a very long night.

All of a sudden the lights clicked on. "Oh, Annie, I thought I heard voices. Why are you sitting here in the dark?" It was Miss Moore. Of all the rotten luck. "Is anything wrong?"

"No, we're fine. That is, my mother wasn't feeling well." I looked at Billy. He had that silly grin back on his face. "We're just giving her a little time to catch her breath."

None of my signals were working. My uncle plunged right ahead. "I'm William Howard, Annie's uncle."

Criminy! *William.* I mean, really. Uncle Billy was too much.

"Nice to meet you." Miss Moore gave him one of her

sweetest smiles and did her little pirouette thing. "And you, too, Mrs. Howard."

Mama looked up and waggled her fingers in response. I wanted to drop through the floor. Her hair had come down on one side and hung across her face in damp strings. Still, she managed a weak half-smile.

"I'd better get back," said Miss Moore. "Hope to see you all again." And she floated out of the room.

Uncle Billy made little soft noises. "Now that's one classy gal."

"I hate to interrupt your drooling, but we need to get Mama home." I was struggling to pin up her wild hair before we risked making a dash for the parking lot.

All the way out to the car, we did our best to keep Mama's legs from folding. When she let out a huge belch, we almost fell down laughing. But we shut up pretty fast when she started making gurgling sounds. Uncle Billy stopped by a row of hedges just in case. "She'd better not lose her dinner on my new seat covers."

"You OK, Mama?" I asked. She gave me a big smile and another burp in return.

We piled into the truck and had to listen to her giggle and hum "It Might as Well Be Spring" the whole ride.

Once we were home, I took Mama into my room and helped her get ready for bed. Daddy was asleep, and it wasn't worth your life to wake him up. Plus I'd heard him cough most of the night before and knew he didn't need being jolted awake. I gathered up some blankets and went into the living room to sleep on the sofa. Billy was there slouched in the old rocking chair.

"This evening's been loads of fun, hasn't it?" he said with a grunt and held out his hands for a blanket. "You going to sleep out here?" Uncle Billy took over making up a bed, tucking in the corners and smoothing everything out. "Now, if my sergeant saw that, he'd be able to bounce a quarter off it. C'mon in the kitchen with me. If there's still enough of a fire, I'll make us some hot chocolate."

Later we sat at the kitchen table over lukewarm cups of cocoa and talked about Mama. "She was awfully quiet tonight," I said. "She hardly said two words."

"At least she's a quiet drunk," said Billy. He stopped to nibble on a piece of ginger snap that was still wearing a sprinkling of pocket fuzz.

"Really, Billy, that's not a very nice thing to say — to call her a drunk." I wasn't at all happy with Mama at the moment, but I didn't like Billy being mean.

"Sorry. You know, until tonight I can't remember ever seeing your mama with too much to drink." Billy took a bite out of another cookie. His pockets must have held an endless supply. "Wonder what set her off?"

I didn't want to tell him what I suspected. That maybe Mr. Gardenia Man had taken her out to dinner after work. Maybe even dropped her off at school. For some reason she'd decided, even after too many drinks, she ought to show up.

"At least she sobered up enough to realize she was making a fool out of herself." I picked at the milk skin settling in on my cocoa. "Something's going on with her. I thought once the shop opened she'd feel settled. Ever since we moved from Seattle, she's seemed so out of sorts."

"See, that's the part I can't figure out," said Billy. He thrust both hands into his pockets and leaned back in his chair. "She was real excited about this move, especially after she found a place for her shop that she and Ma could afford. Don't look at me like that — I know Ma is part of this deal. Anyway, once my buddy told me about this house, it was your mama who convinced Eddie this would be the best chance to have a house of their own. The perfect set-up."

"I remember what it was like when we found out Daddy was really coming home. That he was still alive. That was enough. I didn't give one thought to what it would be like for him — or for Mama."

"You were just a kid. No one expected you to figure out what they were having trouble working out for themselves."

The fire had died down in the stove and the room had turned cold, but neither one of us moved. Uncle Billy stayed quiet for a moment before he said any more. He took my cup and his and went to put them in the sink. "When I first came back, I didn't know where I was most of the time. I mean, I didn't know how to put the war behind me and start over. I put a foot wrong just about every time I moved. It's a wonder your grandma still speaks to me."

"I remember, Billy. I was there."

"Your dad and I never talk much about the war anymore, but right after he got back we needed to talk about it; half the time neither of us knew what we were doing. He told me more than once he was afraid that the best days of his life were over. That the war, that flying, had given him purpose. A sense of pride. But he came home to a wife who'd gotten used to being on her own. With his eyesight gone — well, that's when I knew I'd stick around as long as he needed me." Billy reached over and touched my cheek. "You're growing into a real smart young lady."

When we stood up, he did something he hadn't done in years. He gave me a big hug. "We'll figure things out together, Annie. I promise." Then he got that big old grin on his face again. "Of course, you have to promise you'll talk me up to that Miss Moore."

I gave him a little shove. "Billy, you can be such a goof!"

Later I lay awake thinking about one afternoon years ago when I lived at Grandma's in Walla Walla. Uncle Billy had made it real difficult to love him, and that day right out in front of the library when I'd hugged him as tight as I could, he surprised me by hugging me right back. He'd been home from the war for a year, but I knew he was about the loneliest, most unhappy soul in the world. Just thinking about that day and how far Billy had come since then made me feel hopeful about Daddy. As for Mama, I figured I'd better keep my thoughts to myself.

Chapter 6

Mama was already dressed for work and busy in the kitchen when I got up. I'd spent a restless night on the sofa and woke up thinking about all those nights I'd slept on the unpredictable Murphy bed at Grandma's in Walla Walla, afraid it might suddenly slap right back up into the wall. Made me wish for one of Grandma's banana splits and a good long talk. Mama frowned on long distance calls, but it had been ages since I'd heard from Grandma Hattie. Just thinking about her made me feel less cranky.

"Annie," said Mama. "Did you fold up your blankets and put them away?"

It was just like her to get all bossy before I had a chance to say a word. Her bad mood didn't bother me all that much. It was her way of letting me know she wasn't going to take any sass from me, even though she'd earned it.

While I was folding the blankets, I planned out in my head

what I wanted to say to her, but when I went back to the kitchen Daddy was there.

"Your mama tells me you talked her into going to sleep in your room last night so she wouldn't wake me." Daddy reached for me, and I went to stand by his chair. "That was real thoughtful, honey." He felt for something in the chair next to him. "Here's a little something I thought you'd like to have. I had Ma send it over from Walla Walla."

It was a small, leather-bound sketchbook, with a clasp like a diary. "Oh, Daddy," I said, running my hand over the leather, soft as Mama's kidskin gloves. "This is the best." I gave his arm a squeeze, but the look on Mama's face was enough to make me slip it quickly into my cardigan pocket.

"How's your cold, Daddy?" I asked, giving Mama one of my best squint-eyed looks.

"I'm much better, probably because I had that good long sleep last night." Daddy pulled me closer for a hug, and I bent down and gave him a kiss on the cheek. "There are some of your mama's popovers in the oven, and it's not even my birthday."

I wasn't about to look at Mama again. After she'd humiliated me in front of Miss Moore, I wasn't going to act like nothing had happened. Plus, she drove me mad when she acted all goody-goody like nothing was wrong.

Before I could give her another look, fiercer than the first one, there was a soft little knock at the back door.

It was Ella Mae Hinkle from next door, all bundled up in an ancient furry coat with her hair in its usual mile-high mass of matted curls, the occasional ones springing from her head like antennae. She looked like a cartoon insect. Uncle Billy was convinced she had spiders hiding in that hair. And once the blizzard had passed and we could see into her living room again, we'd noticed she had some kind of peculiar critter sitting on her piano. Billy and I waggled our fingers at it, but the thing never moved.

One Sunday when the Hinkles left for church, we scooted across to their front lawn. "That thing looks an awful lot like a dead cat." Billy had his nose right up to the bay window. "A stuffed dead cat. You don't suppose she's gone and . . . Naw, couldn't be." He shook his head and shooed me back across the lawn.

And now here she was at our door looking an awful lot like that scruffy mystery animal resting on her piano.

"Sorry to trouble you folks," she said, "but I need to use your phone."

"Has yours gone on the blink?" said Mama.

"Oh, no, dearie," said Mrs. Hinkle, "you know, we don't own one. The Mister won't have one of those contraptions in the house."

"Is there something wrong? Can we help?" said Mama. She

motioned to me to take the popovers out of the oven.

"I need to call my sister-in-law. Harry won't come out of his room." Mrs. Hinkle took in a big breath and gave Daddy's popovers a big long look. "My, don't those look good."

Before that old lady had a chance to get her mitts on our breakfast, Uncle Billy rushed into the kitchen from the garage. He came to a full stop when he saw our visitor.

"Billy," said Mama, "I think you need to go with Ella Mae and see if you can help her. She's concerned about her husband." Mama was using her drill sergeant voice again.

"Well, he usually won't pay no mind to anyone but his sister." Mrs. Hinkle's voice kind of trailed off. "And ever since our son Hal came home from the war, Harry don't listen to him either." I noticed she still had her eye on the popovers.

Ordinarily, Uncle Billy didn't take orders from Mama all that seriously, but on this particular morning, I think his curiosity got the better of him.

"C'mon, neighbor," he said. "I'll take you back home and see what Harry is up to." He gave us a wink and Daddy a playful whack on the shoulder.

"My Mister surely does like popovers." Mrs. Hinkle looked ready to pounce.

Mama pressed her lips together to stifle a giggle and quickly wrapped four of the rolls in a clean dishtowel. Ella Mae polished one off in three big bites before she and Billy were even out the door.

Once they were gone, Mama started laughing until she had to wipe the tears away with a corner of her apron. "Well, I never," she said, putting her hand in Daddy's. "And that wild nest of hair, Eddie. You have to wonder what in the world she has stuffed in there."

"Rats' nests and spider webs, if we're to believe Billy," said Daddy. And he doubled over in a burst of laughter he'd most likely been holding in the whole time. Just as quickly, his laughter stopped. "We really should be ashamed of ourselves. We could be a bit more understanding. That poor woman, all this time thinking her son really has come home from the war. I believe Hal was barely nineteen when he went missing."

That made us all quiet for a while. I imagine everyone was thinking about how close Daddy came to not coming home.

"My land," said Mama, looking at her watch, "we'd better get moving. I'm going to be late for work, and you're going to be late for school." All my plans to make a fuss about last night had flown away with Ella Mae Hinkle.

Just then Uncle Billy got back from next door, and he started us laughing all over again with a crazy story about coaxing Harry out of his room with the promise of popovers.

"That old coot was all suited up in a raggedy army uniform. World War I, I expect. Said his missus wouldn't let him have his gun. Claims he's ready to get him some Russkies, and he can't move without his rifle. Poor old guy. He's probably trying to relive his glory days." Billy grabbed his keys and a popover. "Sure hope that gun's in his imagination as well. A couple of characters, the two of them. C'mon, I'll give you both a ride."

I grabbed my coat and my books and gave Daddy a good-bye hug. He was already glued to his radio with a box of screws in his lap, ready to sort them by size into a row of chipped custard dishes. I started for the door and then turned back. Today of all days, I wasn't leaving without giving Daddy a second hug. "Go on now, you're going to be late," he said, but I could tell he was pleased.

Couldn't help but wonder as the three of us squeezed into the pickup if Mama even remembered the night before and the ride home. All the way to school, Billy talked about the mess that was the Hinkles' house. We couldn't get a word in edgewise.

"And you wouldn't believe the collection of junk in that house. A big fat cat on every surface not covered with one thing and another. And that is a dead cat on her ancient piano. She's clearly had it stuffed. Do you suppose it's one of her former pets? And yes, the holiday decorations are still up."

When we got to the edge of the baseball field, I told Billy to drop me off. Didn't want anyone to see me getting out of the pickup, in case someone had seen our graceful little threesome the night before.

Billy had barely come to a stop when I jumped out in the middle of listening to Mama's list of my after-school chores. Before I got very far, Uncle Billy called me over to his side of the truck. "Tell your Miss Moore hello for me," he said, and that big silly grin flashed across his face again. "Tell her what a splendid fellow I am."

I reached in and grabbed his nose. "You wish." What would Billy have to say to Mama the rest of the way? For sure no more Ella Mae Hinkle stories. I hoped he was going to give her several pieces of his mind.

Chapter 7

Johannes was so unlike any boy I'd ever met. It wasn't just his accent and that big smile or those floppy blue pants he sometimes wore. Behind those dreamy blue eyes was a sadness that didn't go with his easy manner. But what did I know about him, really? He could have been in the Communist youth corps for all I knew. Mr. Raymond was always going on about how he could sniff out a Red in two seconds flat, and he seemed really happy about having Johannes in class. I figured I was safe enough getting to know Johannes. He'd said to call him Jon, but I liked to say his full name. Johannes sounded foreign and exotic, like something out of a Charles Boyer film.

I could think of a dozen things I wanted to ask him. But I couldn't very well walk up to him and say, "Tell me, Johannes, how did you get that terrible scar?" Or, "It must have been awful to have Nazis all over the place." Maybe start with how he and Elisabeth got to Tacoma, of all places in the world.

I certainly hoped they hadn't seen Uncle Billy and me practically dragging Mama out to the car after the Parents' Night disaster. And, since I didn't show up at the reception for some of their auntie's cakes, they might think I was stuck-up.

The next Monday I could hardly wait until social studies to see Johannes again, but at the same time, I dreaded it. What if he didn't talk to me — not one word? Anyway, first I had to get through algebra. I hadn't even looked at the homework. When I finally stumbled into class, I was never so glad to see a substitute. He spent the whole hour on the mathematical "beauty" of card games. Criminy!

In art class Miss Moore seemed to float around even more than usual, all excited about us drawing portraits of each other. I ended up being paired with snotty, nose-in-the-air Marlene Joyner, who was convinced she looked like Elizabeth Taylor. She never looked at me once, just made endless sketches of Montgomery Clift from a movie magazine she had stashed in her book bag. Miss Moore's floating came to an abrupt end when a row of shelves fell off the wall, scattering paints and art supplies in all directions.

"Little Miss Kiss-Up," Marlene hissed when I got up to go help.

My good deeds almost made me late for social studies, which I wasn't going to miss for anything. Racing to make class, I saw Johannes and Elisabeth before they saw me. They were both standing outside the social studies classroom.

"Annie," chirped Elisabeth. "We've been waiting for you." She did her little skipping dance. "My Tante Dee," she began, taking in a big breath, "would like you and your mama at our house for tea." She let out a gasp, like she'd been underwater for several seconds and had just come up for air.

"I'll have to check," I said. Oh joy! Johannes must have talked about me at home. Why else would we be invited to tea? But my excitement quickly wilted. Taking Mama would be a disaster. She'd say all the wrong things and be all huffy about something. I could just hear her: "Now who are these people again?"

"What day did you have in mind?" I was hoping it wouldn't be Monday, Mama's day off. In my head I was trying to figure out all the ways I could convince her not to go, without her turning the whole invitation sour.

Johannes looked at his sister. She looked puzzled for a minute. "Next week one day," she said.

"Here is our number for your mother to call." Johannes handed me a slip of paper with a phone number written in bold, block numbers. "She can tell my Tante which day is good."

The final bell rang, and Elisabeth scurried off to gym. Johannes seemed relieved to go to his seat. Was he glad that his aunt had asked us? I would have to think long and hard about what to do. Maybe I could take Daddy instead or even Uncle Billy. Picturing my uncle balancing a teacup on his knee and eating little iced cakes made me giggle. I looked over at Johannes, but he was all business. What if he truly hated the idea?

After class the two of us walked down to the end of the hall together, not a word between us. Every so often he'd move just a smidge closer so that our arms touched. Once his elbow grazed mine, and I felt a little tingle up my arm — probably just my crazy bone.

At the shop class door, he turned with a shrug and said, "Now I go to make birdhouses." He sighed. "Child's work."

"We could switch. You can make the world's ickiest pudding, blancmange, and I'll make a birdhouse."

Johannes got very quiet and frowned. Finally, he smiled, "I see, you have made a joke." He reached over and pushed a strand of hair out of my eyes. "Funny word, blancmange."

"It's a perfectly nauseating dessert, and you're welcome to it." My heart had started to pound again, so my words came out in a breathless rush. The bell rang and saved me from embarrassing myself. When Johannes took my hand, I felt a flutter in my stomach.

"See you later, no?" he said, and let go of my hand.

"See you later, yes," I said, and floated across the hall to home ec as effortlessly as Miss Moore.

It was my turn to be on clean-up duty, so I had to scrub leftover pudding off a zillion slimy plates before I could leave class. I wasn't the only one who couldn't stomach blancmange. By the time I finished each slimy, yucky dish, Johannes was long gone from shop class. I was on my way to my locker when Miss Moore caught up with me.

"If you aren't in a hurry to get home, could you come down to my room after school? I need to talk to you," she said, drifting by me in a vapor trail of scarves.

Any time a teacher had asked me to stay after class, I was certain it meant trouble. I couldn't imagine what I'd done. By the time I reached the classroom door, my heart was about to jump out of my chest. I knocked softly, even though the door was already open.

"Come in," Miss Moore said over her shoulder. She was stacking the rest of the fallen books and supplies on one of the work tables. "What a mess. I need a first-rate carpenter to get these shelves back up and make sure they'll stay up."

I tried to swallow a snicker and thought I'd covered it up with a cough.

"Something funny, Annie?"

"No ma'am — that is, my uncle and my father are both carpenters." What I didn't say was that one of those carpenters would be overjoyed to fix those shelves.

"Well, I may need their help, but I didn't ask you here to

talk about bookshelves." Miss Moore motioned me to a desk at the front of the room. "Sit down, Annie." And then she moved a jar full of brushes on her desk and perched on the edge, the little mirrors on her skirt flashing tiny beams of light.

My mind was racing, and my mouth was all dry. What in the world did she want? She was smiling, so whatever it was couldn't be too bad.

"You know, Annie," she said, holding up my sketch of snotty Marlene, "this is really very good."

I felt my cheeks go warm. No one had ever said anything like that to me before. Well, Grandma Hattie always had nice things to say, but after all, she was my grandmother. Thank goodness Miss Moore didn't wait for an answer.

"I believe you have real talent, and I hoped you could start working with me after school, say a couple afternoons a week. The all-city art contest is coming up, and I'd like to see if you can't have something ready to submit." She studied the drawing some more. "I'd like to get you started on watercolor. I have a feeling that you'll be a natural in that medium."

I finally found my voice. "Thank you," I said softly. "But I'm not sure I have any afternoons free. I'll have to check with my mother."

Miss Moore braced herself on her hands and leaned forward. "Surely, for something as important as this, she could spare you a couple of hours a week?"

"Maybe." I didn't want to say what I was thinking. Mama would think of a million reasons why art lessons after school were just plain silly. Besides, there was Daddy.

"Perhaps I should call your parents first." Miss Moore had this big old smile on her face like that was the best idea yet. "Of course, that's what I should do."

If she only knew. "Thanks, but I'll talk to them and let you know first thing tomorrow. Promise." I jumped up from the desk and grabbed my stuff and hurried out of the room.

When I got to the front hall, Johannes and his sister were leaning against the lockers. "We have been waiting for you," said Elisabeth. "To give you a ride home. Our uncle is here to take us."

As soon as we stepped outside, an enormous dark Lincoln pulled up and stopped in front of us. A man with round rosy cheeks got out and, with a tip of his cap, motioned me to the back seat.

"Our Uncle Hendrik picks us up some days when he must take the car out," said Johannes.

Johannes and Elisabeth climbed in the back seat with me. They were giggling like naughty children. Before I could say a thing, Elisabeth reached into a narrow cabinet built into the back of the front seat and pulled out a basket filled with cookies. She reached into a canvas bag on the floor and brought out three cups and a thermos that turned out to be full of hot chocolate. I was speechless.

A little window between us and the driver's seat slid back. "No *kruimels*," said Uncle Hendrik, addressing the rearview mirror.

"Crumbs," whispered Johannes, his blue eyes sparkling like crazy. Then he leaned into the little window and said something in Dutch I couldn't understand. He and his uncle both started laughing. And what else could I do but laugh as well . . . what with finding myself in the back of a limousine full of *kruimels* and on my way to being a world-famous artist.

Chapter 8

When the grand car stopped in front of our house, Uncle Hendrik jumped out and made a great show of opening my door. I could swear I heard his heels click. Switching to sit in the front seat, Johannes stopped to give my hand a squeeze. I felt a little dizzy watching them drive off.

The curtains twitched at Mrs. Hinkle's. She'd most likely make a beeline for our back door the first chance she got, pretending she needed sugar or an egg. I was halfway up the walk when our front door flew open and Grandma Hattie hurried down the steps to meet me, her face a wreath of smiles.

"My land, Sweetpea," she said, giving me a big hug, "who brought you home, Lady Astor?"

I hugged Grandma right back and held her tight, hoping she'd feel just how glad I was to see her and how much we needed her good common sense to set things straight. On the way up the walk, I kept my arm around her waist, and she'd stop every so often to give me another kiss on the cheek.

"Grandma, I'm so glad you're here."

"I'm glad to hear it, milady," she said with a little bow, "but I have only my humble Ford to offer you." She pulled me into a hug again, and I walked up the steps and into the front hall, ready to burst with all the things I had to tell her.

"Tell me," said Grandma, after she'd settled herself in Daddy's chair by the kitchen stove, "has a rich relative I don't know about died and left you a fortune?"

"Of course not. It's even better."

I was glad we were alone — Daddy and Billy were most likely in the workshop — because finally I could tell someone all about Johannes — and Elisabeth. Grandma wouldn't tease or make fun, so I filled her in on what little I knew about them and the war and living with their aunt and uncle, although I left out the part about how my heart fluttered and skipped a beat every time Johannes got near me.

"And you'll get a chance to meet them because I'm invited to tea and you can come with me." Perfect, I thought. "You are staying for a few days, aren't you, Grandma?"

"Of course," she said. "I wouldn't miss any of this excitement for the world."

We sat at the kitchen table over cups of tea and talked. I wanted to tell her about Mama, that I had begun to worry because she and Daddy seemed so far apart, but I just couldn't find the words. I did tell her about Miss Moore and the art lessons.

"My land," she said, "I think that's a fine idea. Must be a bit of your grandpa's talent. He could draw anything he put his mind to." Grandma reached over and patted my arm. "Sweetpea, take Miss Moore up on her offer. It's a grand opportunity. Don't worry so much about taking care of everybody else. Billy and your daddy will be fine on their own a couple of days a week."

The back door rattled, and when I went to see who was there, I found Mrs. Hinkle with a battered tin cup in her hand. She had on that awful furry coat again, and something seemed to be crawling around under her collar. "Could you spare a cup of cream, sweetie?" Her collar moved again. She patted it down and moved away, clearly to have a better view into the kitchen. "Got company, honey? I saw that fancy car drop you off. You must be traveling in mighty high cotton to get a ride home in a car like that."

Grandma had come to the back door to see what was going on. I introduced them, and Grandma kept Mrs. Hinkle occupied while I went for the cream. I figured I'd better wash out the cup. It had a coating of something grimy, like maybe it had been out in the garden for days. When I returned, Mrs. Hinkle thanked me and only left the porch when Grandma told her she had a cake in the oven.

"A cup of cream, my foot," said Grandma. "That woman was just nosing around for some good gossip. What a character! And what was that slinking around under her collar? I hope I'm mistaken, but it might have been a mouse or even a rat. I suppose it could have been a kitten." Grandma gave a little shiver and watched Mrs. Hinkle go through the crooked gate between our yards. "My stars, that woman just tossed the cream. Tells you something, doesn't it?"

"She's the nosiest old thing. I should have told her we were out of cream. And I wouldn't put it past her to have a pet rat. Billy says she has a stuffed cat in her living room, not to mention the bats in her belfry."

We had a good laugh and were just coming to our senses when Daddy and Uncle Billy came into the kitchen from the workshop.

"Sorry, Ma," said Uncle Billy. "We didn't mean to take so long, but Howard Brothers Fine Carpentry has its first job — a cradle for an old army buddy."

It was Mama's late night, so we all pitched in for dinner, and when the dishes were done, Daddy and Uncle Billy went back out to the workshop. Grandma phoned Mrs. VanderVelde, and we were all set for tea the very next afternoon right after school. And later Mama didn't bat an eye when we told her about our afternoon plans for the next day. Grandma heated up some leftovers for Mama, and the two of them spent the rest of the evening talking about the new shop. I didn't say another word about Miss Moore.

Uncle Billy had drawn us a little map to get to the Vander-Veldes, but I was certain we had the wrong place. Surely, they didn't live in a mansion. And that exclusive girl's school, Annie Wright's Seminary, so close by. This was a neighborhood of rolling lawns like plush green carpets and Cadillacs parked in mile-long driveways.

"Astonishing," said Grandma, when we pulled into the VanderVeldes' driveway. "Look at that house and that garden. And all those rhododendrons. Imagine what it must look like when they're in full bloom."

Johannes and his uncle were waiting for us at the end of the driveway. Grandma stopped near a row of hedges and decided to leave the car there.

Uncle Hendrik came over and opened our doors. "Good! Good!"

Grandma looked at me. "Must mean we leave the car here." We got out and followed right behind him. Johannes ran up ahead.

Instead of entering the elegant mansion, Uncle Hendrik and Johannes led us around the garage to a small cottage that was a miniature version of the main house.

Dee VanderVelde came out of the front door, wiping her hands on her apron. "Welcome," she said. "Welcome."

We all ended up in the kitchen, except for Uncle Hendrik, who had to finish polishing the car. The room was full of the smell of cinnamon and some other dreamy spice I couldn't recognize. Elisabeth was making cookies that she rolled over a wooden spoon handle before popping into the oven.

Grandma and Mrs. VanderVelde acted like long-lost friends and were soon talking about apple cobblers and homemade bread. Elisabeth shooed Johannes and me into the living room where a fire crackled in the fireplace, even though it was only four o'clock in the afternoon. The light threw bobbing, crazy quilt patterns on the ceiling. I felt like I was in an enchanted cottage. The walls were a soft yellow and full of blue and white plates hung like pictures. Johannes took my hand and led me to a large sofa piled high with soft pillows.

He picked up a cigar box from a side table and sat down next to me. Johannes opened the lid and took out a small square photo. "Here is my mama and papa with little Elisabeth. See there, in the background. That is me standing like a little soldier. Such a face!"

"You don't look very happy," I said.

"How angry I was," Johannes said with a smile. "Papa had just spanked me for shoving Elisabeth." He hesitated and the smile faded. "Now she is all I have left of home."

Johannes put down the picture. The room was quiet, just the murmur of voices in the background coming from the kitchen. I wanted to say how sorry I was, but my throat had turned to sandpaper. I wanted to touch his face, but my arms stayed frozen to my sides. Besides, nothing I could say would be enough to take away that sadness in his eyes. I just knew that something terrible had happened to his mother and father during the war.

He took both my hands in his. "I am so glad you come to tea today," he said. We sat there, our hands clasped together, the warmth from his hands rushing to my face. My heart raced. My ears buzzed. Suddenly he stood up and pulled me into a hug. And then he kissed me, a gentle kiss, no more than a butterfly touching my lips. Without even thinking, I kissed him right back, not a butterfly in sight.

Chapter 9

"Hand me another one of those little puffball things, would you, Sweetpea?" said Grandma. "Those really do melt in your mouth."

Mrs. VanderVelde had given us a box of pastries to take home, but we'd already raided it twice before we'd driven half a mile. It was a wonder I could eat a thing. I'd barely touched a mouthful the whole afternoon. Somehow I'd turned into one of those dopey girls who go all moony over boys. But I couldn't help it. Every time Johannes looked at me, I practically choked. At one point Elisabeth thumped me on the back and turned and gave Johannes a little slap on the knee. Did she know? She hadn't said anything, but she did give me a wink when Johannes reached under the table and took my hand while the tea was being poured. I wasn't going to think about any of it now. Maybe later, alone in my room, I'd celebrate my first kiss and remember those blue eyes and the way they caught fire like sparklers. I'd drool into my pillow, away from prying eyes. But I just wasn't going to go all dreamy now. My face would get all hot and flushed and Grandma wouldn't rest until she'd heard every last detail.

Suddenly, she braked hard. "Honestly, you'd think when everyone put their cars on blocks during the war, they forgot how to drive. That fellow pulled right out in front of me." One handed, Grandma wrestled a hanky out of her purse and brushed at the sprinkling of powdered sugar that clung to her mouth and lay like fine dust on the lapels of her coat. "Let's see if we can get the rest of the way downtown to pick up your mama without someone doing something crazy." And with that, Grandma crossed in front of a whole line of cars to make a left turn. Horns blared, but she ignored them.

"Nice family, those VanderVeldes," said Grandma, when the noise had died down. "They certainly landed on their feet coming to Tacoma. I wouldn't want to be at the beck and call of other folks, but Dee tells me, despite the fact that Hendrik was a lawyer in Holland, they count themselves lucky to have such pleasant work. Been through a lot, especially your friend Jon and his sister. He's certainly sweet on you."

"I like him a lot, Grandma." My voice was barely a whisper.

Grandma reached over and patted my hand. "I can tell you do, sweetie, but you best go slow. From what little his aunt told me, I figure he's lived more lives than you could imagine. What those two kids need most right now is a really good friend. And you can be that friend."

I squeezed Grandma's hand. How could I explain what was going on in my heart when I didn't know what to make of it myself? I touched my fingers to my lips and wondered if maybe I'd only imagined that kiss.

When we got to the shop, Mama was already waiting for us at the curb. She was bubbling over with excitement. I jumped out and pushed the seat forward so I could get into the back. "You'll never guess who came into the shop today," Mama said, not waiting for an answer. "The mayor's wife, Mrs. John Daniel Key herself. Just walked in. No appointment. Of course I fit her in."

Mama was so excited her words came out in a rush, and she stayed on the curb babbling until Grandma motioned her to get in. There was a crunch of gears and the car lurched forward into traffic and we started home. Mama was still talking. I was sure any minute she'd turn blue and slide off the seat onto the floor.

"And another thing," she stopped to catch her breath. "Mrs. Key said she'd recommend me to her garden club, that she'd been looking for the longest time for someone who could do her hair the way she liked it. Her style's a bit out of date, but I'm willing to do whatever she wants, as long as it brings her back."

No one got a word in all the way home. Mama was still going on about the mayor's wife when we pulled into the driveway and came to a grinding halt. After a solid fifteen minutes listening about Mrs. Mayor, I could have picked her out in a crowd. I reached for the pastries and made a dash for the kitchen, leaving Mama still jabbering away at poor Grandma.

Daddy and Uncle Billy had their own excitement. I was barely in the back door when I heard Daddy yelling for me to come into the living room. "Come look at this beauty. It's about the finest work I've done — well, we've done."

The cradle stood in the bay window, a bed fit for a princess right out of a fairy tale. The basket hung between two hand-carved stands, the finish practically glowing. Daddy and Uncle Billy gleamed as well.

"It's absolutely beautiful," I said. "It even smells good."

Daddy ran his hand over the spindles. "I expect it's the beeswax; that's what gives the wood such a beautiful finish."

Uncle Billy took my hand. "Here, run your fingers over that. Smooth as silk."

I thought of the treasure box with the butterfly inlay on the top Billy had made me so long ago. He and Daddy could both work magic with wood.

"What are you all doing in here with all that fine pastry in the kitchen?" Grandma burst into the room, with Mama close on her heels. "My, is that the new cradle? What a lovely piece of work."

Mama barely gave the cradle a glance. "Eddie, I've got the greatest news. You'll never guess what."

I could see Daddy's face fall. "What is it, Dorothy?"

And then Mama launched into the tale of the mayor's wife again. Grandma took this as her signal to move back to the kitchen and the VanderVelde pastries. Uncle Billy went with her. And still Mama went on without a word about the cradle. One look at Daddy told me any minute steam might shoot out of his ears. My stomach did a couple of flips, waiting for the blow-up. I didn't have to wait long.

"You know, Dorothy," said Daddy, "I don't give a damn about that shop of yours or the mayor's wife." He kicked a chair out of the way and stumbled out of the room.

Mama turned and gave me a look.

"Honestly, Mama," I said, my insides still pitching and rolling, "Daddy was waiting for you to say something about the new cradle he and Billy just finished."

"Oh, that," said Mama unpinning her hat. "It is nice, but your dad has always been clever with wood, Billy too. Now, don't give me one of your looks. I'll go change my clothes and then talk to him."

I left Mama in the living room and went looking for Daddy. Grandma and Uncle Billy were in the kitchen laughing over glasses of buttermilk. Two apple pastries were left in the box.

"I know, Sweetpea, we've gone and spoiled our dinner," said Grandma. "But it was worth it." Another burst of laughter.

Seems like they didn't know a thing about the fireworks in the living room. Grandma and Billy were having too much fun. Normally, Daddy's anger would have caught their attention for sure. Where in the world had he gotten to? Best not to worry anyone, so I didn't say a word.

Billy took a swipe at his mouth with his sleeve. "That jelly roll thing was a treat. Maybe that Mrs. VanderVelde would come cook for us."

I looked at the smudges of buttermilk on the inside of Billy's glass and turned away. "I don't know how you can drink that stuff. It's awful. Makes me gag." The state I was in, it was a wonder I didn't upchuck one of those pastry things right there on the kitchen floor.

"You don't know what you're missing," said Grandma as she picked up both their glasses, rinsed them out, and put them in the dishpan. "I suppose we should be thinking about dinner."

"Don't worry, Ma. I'll run out to Busch's and get us some burgers. My treat."

"I'll go with you, son. I want to get a paper, and my car is blocking your truck anyway." Grandma gave me a quick peck on the cheek. "Go tell your mama and daddy where we're going and then set the table. We'll be back in a jiffy."

"Any idea where Daddy is?"

Uncle Billy looked at Grandma. "He's out in the living room, isn't he?"

"Last I knew." Grandma picked up her purse and started for the back door. "He could be out in the workshop, but then we didn't see him come through here." Billy shook his head.

Daddy wasn't in the bedroom. Mama was changing her clothes and said she hadn't seen him. He wasn't in the workshop. I couldn't imagine where he'd gone. It was too dark and cold for him to be wandering around outside by himself, but I grabbed my old corduroy jacket and searched the yard anyway.

"Hey, missy." It was Mrs. Hinkle calling me from her front porch. I wondered if I could pretend I hadn't heard her, but no such luck. "You looking for your daddy?"

"Yes, ma'am." That woman was such a pest.

"Well, he's over here, sampling some of my homemade sauerkraut."

I went up the Hinkles' front steps wondering if I'd heard her right. Ever since the war, Daddy couldn't stomach sauerkraut or anything with boiled cabbage. But sure enough, I followed Mrs. Hinkle through the dozens of boxes and bric-a-brac that filled both the front room and the dining room, and there he was, big as life, in her kitchen with a bowl of sauerkraut in front of him. An orange cat sat on the edge of the table washing his paw — I wondered if he'd been sampling the sauerkraut, too — and a large gray tabby looked down from the top of the fridge.

"Gee, Daddy, I've been looking everywhere for you."

"And here I am." Daddy got up from the table. "Thank you, ma'am, for your hospitality. Tell Harry I was sorry to miss him."

Outside, Daddy took my arm, and we made our way slowly down the porch steps.

"Let's not go home just yet. Let's walk a bit."

"What in the world were you doing there, Daddy?"

"Well, I had to get out of the house, and once I got outside, I thought, where in the world am I going to go? And then *she* came along, said she thought I was her Hal, poor old thing, and practically dragged me up those stairs." Daddy shivered. "Insisted I had to have some of her homemade sauerkraut. An old family recipe — you bet, one that includes several parts cat hair." Daddy stuck out his tongue and shook his head. "I mostly pushed the fork around."

"I'd stay clear of that kitchen if I were you, Daddy."

"Pretty bad, huh?"

"Really nasty!"

"Should we walk as far as Wolfe's Market?"

"If you want. Grandma and Billy went to get hamburgers."

"I need a few more minutes to cool off."

"The cradle is really beautiful, Daddy. Mama was just excited about her day. I know she can be a pain sometimes, but she wants to make a success of that shop. She's worked hard." No response. We walked in silence for a while.

"We must be near the bus stop by now," said Daddy. "Let's sit a while. You're not cold, are you?"

I steered him to the bench. "We should go back soon. Grandma and Billy are probably home by now." I didn't bring up Mama again.

"It's funny, my girl, how all your life you think you know what you want, and then one day you're not even sure of any of it anymore. Makes a fellow reconsider a lot of things." He patted my hand. "I'd like to believe I can do whatever I've a mind to. Maybe I should make some inquiries about the Blinded Veterans Association. My buddy was real keen on getting me involved. I need to make your mama proud of me again, get around more, take better care of you, be more help to Billy."

"You take care of us just fine, Daddy, but I bet there's new things, too. All kinds of things for you to do and others just waiting for you to learn about."

"Learn something new? I don't know. Maybe I'm too old."

"Daddy, don't be silly. You aren't that old."

"It might mean me going away, you know. Maybe for several weeks, months even. I'd miss you like the dickens."

I hadn't thought about Daddy leaving — that to get more help, he'd have to leave us. A big old rock went kerplunk straight to my stomach.

Daddy stood up and reached for my hand. "Don't pay any attention to me. I'm just feeling sorry for myself today. Best we go back to the house. I just felt a few drops of rain."

Daddy was proud. It wasn't like him to let me see him down, and his words made me uneasy. I let them churn around in my head for a bit. Then the truth hit me. Of course, to learn to be more independent, he'd have to go away. My insides felt cold and hard. But this was what I'd hoped for Daddy — that he could get more of his old life back. And I'd been pushing Grandma and Billy to help make it happen. But that old rock had landed right smack dab in the pit of my stomach, and I figured it wasn't going to budge for a good long while.

Chapter 10

Of all the dumb things girls can do, going all boy crazy was the one thing I swore I'd never let happen to me. So falling for Johannes caught me completely by surprise. All the other ninth-grade boys were goofs, especially those who still thought boogers were funny and loud belches a laugh riot. Johannes was definitely different.

I found myself dreaming about him, writing his name dozens of times in my notebook, and swooning over the way his eyes sparkled when he got all intense. But most of all, I kept reliving the tingling of that sweet first kiss. I had to pull myself out of that dream world to focus on Daddy. He really needed to feel better about himself. I wasn't sure I had room in my head to stew about both of them. It was a good thing Grandma had showed up. She must have guessed she'd arrived just when we needed her most. She was still there on the weekend and didn't seem to have any plans to go back to Walla Walla real soon.

I found her Sunday morning in the kitchen, a dishtowel pinned to her blouse, making her fabulous French toast. When I came in for breakfast, she plopped a plateful down in front of me. The wood stove was throwing off heat, making the kitchen toasty and Grandma's white hair a frizzy cloud all around her head. The smell of nutmeg and cinnamon with a little maple syrup mixed in filled the room.

"Your mama's off somewhere, but those two lazy boys of mine aren't up yet." Grandma dropped several slices of bacon onto the skillet, where they sputtered and sizzled like a trout on a campfire.

"I wish you could stay forever, Grandma," I said, sprinkling a heap of powdered sugar on my toast. "Your French toast is the best!"

"Well, forever might be more than I can spare, but with Gloria and her Will watching the store for me, I can take my time." She took a corner of the towel and patted at her face. "Remember their Lily is nearly a year old now, so they have their hands full. She is the sweetest little pixie, but she can be a mischief-maker, too."

If Gloria, Grandma's bookkeeper, hadn't been my closest friend the year I spent in Walla Walla, I would have suffered from real serious honest-to-goodness homesickness. Gloria had married Willie Dupree, the soldier who'd accompanied Daddy home from the war. After Lily was born, they figured Willie and Lily might be a bit much, so now it was plain Will.

"Maybe I'll come over next summer. I miss Gloria, and I can't wait to meet Lily."

"Since you didn't make it over last year," said Grandma, filling a plate for herself, "I think that's a grand plan, and I know Gloria would love having you around."

"Before we make any summer plans for Walla Walla, I need your help convincing Daddy to consider getting out on his own more, maybe applying for a guide dog." If anyone had any influence on him, Grandma Hattie was the one person he wouldn't brush off. But, wouldn't you know it, he took that very moment to come in from the workshop, so Grandma touched his arm and handed him her plate. She gave me a quick nod as if to say, "Later," and began to sprinkle powdered sugar on Daddy's toast.

"My land, son, what time did you go out to the shop?" Grandma said. "I've been up since the crack of dawn. I figured it was just me and your neighbor's raggedy cats stirring."

"Little brother and I've been out there since six-thirty. We have an order for a fancy baby crib." Daddy dug into his breakfast. Grandma sat down next to him and speared a piece of his toast for herself.

I'd barely taken Grandma's place at the stove before Billy rushed in like someone was chasing him. Ever since Howard Brothers Fine Carpentry had started getting orders, he never seemed to plain walk anymore. He had a drawing pad with him and a pencil behind his ear. "I need help," he said, clearing a space for the pad on the table. "I've been out there trying to draw nursery rhyme characters, and I'll be darned if I can get anything right."

"Billy, you're about to dip your drawings in my breakfast." Grandma grabbed her plate. "Bet I know someone who can help you with those." She winked at me.

"Me, too, Ma, but he's been sketching stars and angels for a good many years."

"I don't mean your pa, bless your heart, I'm talking about that young lady who's putting a plate of French toast in front of you."

I felt my face flush and hurried back to the stove.

"Now I should have thought about that. Of course, she must have lots of kids' books I can look at."

Grandma let out a long sigh. "Honestly, Billy, you do try my patience once in a while."

Daddy couldn't help but snicker. "I believe she means our Annie can help you with the drawings, you knucklehead."

I'd already talked to Daddy about Miss Moore's offer to give me extra art lessons, and he was real pleased, but he agreed with me that Mama might not feel the same way. Even though Grandma was doing her best to help things along, none of us had said a thing to Mama.

Later, out in the workshop, I was ready with my box of colored pencils and some drawing paper, but my dear uncle didn't seem real eager to have my help. I pretended I didn't notice and looked through my old fairy tales for illustrations that would give me ideas for the crib. He mumbled and swore under his breath trying to work out his own drawings while I sketched like crazy.

"Well I'll be. Those are really swell," said Billy when I showed him what I'd drawn. "I like the one where you have all the characters marching up to the castle." He held my sketches up to a piece of wood that would become one of the crib end pieces. "This frog in the hat is just the ticket." He gave my shoulders a squeeze. "When in the world did you learn to draw like that? Wow!"

At that I felt my face color several shades of red. "Geez Billy, these are just a few sketches. The hardest part will be figuring out the best way to transfer the drawings onto the wood. Maybe Miss Moore will have some suggestions."

"That's right. And maybe she'd come over and give us some help."

I just had to shake my head and roll my eyes. "For Pete's sake, Billy."

A little later when Daddy joined us, we described our sketches. At first he suggested Billy might carve the figures. We put our heads together and weighed all our ideas. Billy figured that adding more wood would make the crib too heavy. In the end, we finally settled on hand painting them and then sealing the wood. We were a team. Daddy and Billy gushed words of praise on me, and I lapped them up like cream.

Just before noon, Grandma came in and asked us if we were planning on having some lunch. Daddy and Billy went on ahead, but I pulled Grandma aside.

"Grandma, I'm serious. We should at least find out how Daddy can get a guide dog, and I need you to help me convince him."

"My goodness, that's a tall order. It isn't all that simple, Sweetpea. I mean, you don't just go out and get a guide dog like you'd buy a family pet. I mean, I'm pretty sure weeks of training are involved for both the dog and your daddy, but also, I should think, adjustments for the family." Grandma took my hand. "I know you want to help, Annie Leigh, but we need to look into this whole thing before we start making any plans."

I put my arm around Grandma's waist. "We've got to start pretty soon. Daddy's in low spirits, for sure, no matter how he seems to you."

"We'll sit down real soon and thrash all of this out, but for now, your young man is waiting for you in the living room. His uncle didn't bring him. Jon rode over on his bike. He's certainly sweet on you — that's a quick ride in the car. But imagine making it up some of those hills on a bike, for goodness' sake!" Grandma gave my face a pat. "Love is surely in bloom."

Chapter 11

I checked my blouse for any stray maple syrup stains and took a deep breath before walking into the living room. Johannes was sitting in the window seat studying the disgusting satin sweetheart pillow Daddy had sent Mama just before he shipped overseas.

"These words are a poem?" he asked, holding the pillow close to his face for a better look. "Is it *romantisch*?"

"Mama wouldn't call it *romantisch*. 'Absolutely ghastly' were her exact words. That poem is way too lovey-dovey, for sure. Not the perfect farewell gift, but Daddy sent it home with some of his stuff before he went overseas."

All those beautiful hand-stitched cushions at the Vander-Veldes' house. Johannes was going to think we had absolutely no taste.

"It's kind of a family joke now," I said, quickly snatching the icky thing and squishing it inside the cupboard under the seat. "I guess during the war the army figured these were real swell declarations of love. Soldiers sent them home to their wives and girlfriends."

Johannes scrunched up his face, probably wondering how those old generals and colonels could have possibly imagined that a cheap hand-painted pillow with ugly fringe was *romantisch*.

"C'mon, I'm sure my grandmother has lunch waiting for us in the kitchen." I grabbed his hand, but Johannes didn't move.

"You have bicycle?" Johannes asked. "We go for ride together . . . OK?"

"Sure. I have an old bike in the garage." I smiled and squeezed his hand. But those blue eyes weren't sparkling like usual. I wondered what had happened to dull them so completely. Sadness was all I could see.

When we went through the kitchen, I stopped to introduce Johannes to Uncle Billy and Daddy. A plate of filled doughnut-like things sat between them. Flakes of pastry were everywhere, including on their chins.

"So you are the young fellow who brought these terrific treats," said Daddy, wiping at a bit of crumbs in the corners of his mouth. "I'm afraid I've made a pig of myself."

"These apple flapjack things are the best." Uncle Billy grabbed another one and took a giant bite. I prayed he wouldn't rub his stomach and say something stupid like "yum, yum."

That would be the absolute end. For sure Johannes would think we were a family of slobs.

"*Appelflappen*," said Johannes, a silly grin finally lighting up his face. "Not apple jacks."

"Whatever they are, they're darned good." Uncle Billy took another big bite. "You kids had any lunch?"

"Ma left you some ham sandwiches," said Daddy, through a mouthful of pastry.

"We're going for a bike ride; we'll make a picnic out of it." I rushed two sandwiches and a couple of oranges into a lunch bag. Daddy and Uncle Billy might start asking Johannes tons of embarrassing questions if we didn't get going.

Uncle Billy leaned back in his chair. "Bike ride, huh? There's a pump in the garage by the tool closet; you're going to need it. When I walked the old Schwinn out of the garage, Johannes took one look and pointed out the flat back tire, as well as a loose chain.

"I fix," he said, and went out to the front yard where he'd left his bike. Johannes returned with a kind of saddlebag in his hand. Turned out it held a million funny little wrenches and some tire patches. After several minutes of fussing with the chain and pumping up the patched back tire, Johannes rode around the back yard on a test drive. He suddenly let fly a long string of Dutch — cuss words, most likely. He fiddled some more with one of those little wrenches and declared, "OK.

Now we can go."

I wheeled my bike out to the front street, and Johannes followed. "Let's go to Point Defiance. We can go over to Pearl. It will take us right to the park entrance." I buttoned my old pea coat up to the collar. Johannes just stood there staring; he was miles away.

I gave him a poke. "Don't worry. After your ride over here, a trip to the park will be a breeze." I felt in the pocket for my old wool beret. Outside the sky was a dull gray. It would probably rain before we got back.

We almost made it to Point Defiance without stopping, but a cramp in my calf brought me to a quick stop. Just as I was getting off my bike to walk off the pain, a couple of boys from school sailed by. Then they turned back and began to ride circles around us, yelling "Kraut" at Johannes.

"Look, the Kraut has a girlfriend," yelled a chubby, pimply-faced boy, doing a wheelie on his bike to show off. "Must be a dirty Kraut lover."

"You're so stupid. He's Dutch, not German," I yelled back. "You wouldn't know a Nazi if you fell over one."

They circled closer and closer, pointing at Johannes's clothes and yelling ugly things that made me blush. Johannes held up his hand as if to say, "Let me handle this." He grabbed the taller one of the boys, pulled him off his bike, and shoved him over to the curb where he leaned into him until their noses must have been touching. I couldn't hear what he said. The other shorter boy threw himself on Johannes and grabbed his legs, but Johannes raised his arm, and that's when I saw the flash of one of the bike wrenches he had curled in his fist. We all stood there, frozen in place, the only sounds coming from the boys gasping for breath. It must have been only a matter of seconds, but it felt like several minutes. Johannes finally let go of the taller bully, who quickly backed away, a wet stain slowly spreading down his pant leg.

The boys grabbed their bikes and zoomed off, pumping furiously in a burst of speed.

It was a side of Johannes I wasn't sure I wanted to see, but then, those stupid boys had begun to frighten me.

"Bullies! I hate bullies!" he said, spitting out a loud string of words in Dutch for good measure. He didn't need to translate. He just hopped back on his bike and signaled me to get on mine, and we rode off.

We didn't stop to talk about what had happened. I wasn't sure what to say to Johannes at the moment. Every so often he would fly past me, only to slow down if he got too far ahead. He was a speed demon on that fine bike of his, racing away from something I was sure was more than just those dumb boys we'd left behind.

Once inside the park, we leaned our bikes against a tree next to a picnic table by the glider swings. I was breathless from the ride and what had just happened, but I wasn't about to let Johannes see that. I grabbed our lunch out of my basket and handed a sandwich and an orange to Johannes. He had a thermos of hot chocolate in one of those saddlebag things. I wondered if it was some kind of Dutch custom: always have a thermos of hot chocolate handy in case of an emergency.

After nibbling on my ham on rye, I picked up the wax paper and scraps and tossed them into the nearest trashcan. Johannes hadn't touched his sandwich. He sat peeling his orange into perfect strips, only to ignore it. I slipped mine into my pocket.

I sat back down. "Want to check out the zoo?" I said.

Johannes shook his head slowly. "Annie, I must tell you some things." He took a big breath and his voice broke, his eyes glistening. "We hear today . . . " He stopped to look at his shoes. When he looked back up, his cheeks were wet. "My cousin Herman in Holland . . . we know for certain now . . . he died in the war."

I stayed quiet for a moment before I reached across and took Johannes's hand in both of mine. "I'm really sorry."

He leaned over and gently unfolded my hands, kissing the tip of each finger, before placing them, ever so gently, over his heart. I felt lightheaded and a bit flushed, certain he could hear the pounding in my chest. Neither of us moved. I just held tight and watched the tears slide silently down Johannes's cheeks.

Chapter 12

We started the ride back to my house slow and steady. Neither of us were in the mood to race. Every so often we would swerve close to each other and touch hands. Finally, we got off and walked our bikes the last few blocks home.

Parked in front of the house was the grand car, but no sign of Uncle Hendrik. We found him, along with Grandma Hattie, Daddy, and Uncle Billy, in the kitchen having coffee and feasting on big slabs of potato bread fresh out of the oven, laughing and joking like old pals. Grandma was at the stove checking on a loaf in the oven. When she looked up, her eyes twinkled with laughter. She was having a fine time.

"*Hallo Oom*," said Johannes, his face turning Crisco white. "Something . . . it is wrong? Why are you here?"

The room went completely still for about a second.

Uncle Hendrik did a kind of half jump out of his chair. "*Nee!* Not to worry. Everything is tip-top, tip-top."

Clearly, Johannes had been startled by his uncle showing up out of the blue. But his presence didn't mean bad news. In fact, it turned out that he'd been sent to bring me back to their house for dinner. Grandma had a quiet conversation with Uncle Hendrik and Daddy, while I went to change out of my dungarees. I wondered if my invitation had anything to do with Johannes's reaction to the news about his cousin.

The ride to the VanderVeldes' was not the same as the playful drive on our last trip in the car. After struggling to fit Johannes's bicycle into the car's colossal trunk, Uncle Hendrik kept up a constant chatter until we reached the cottage drive-way. We couldn't get a word in edgewise, and Johannes didn't seem to feel like talking anyway. So I just sat quietly next to him and breathed in the sweet scent of Lux soap that clung to his sweater.

No one was around when we arrived. Tante Dee was most likely in the main house fixing dinner.

"Elisabeth is still at her piano lesson, so I'll put on the ket-tle," said Johannes, pulling me along into the kitchen. "Tante Dee should be here soon. We'll have cakes with tea and some music. OK?"

Only he pronounced it "hoo-kay." I started to giggle. "OK," I replied. "Yes, hoo-kay!"

Johannes filled the tea kettle and put it on the stove. On his way out the back door to fetch his aunt, he unlatched the top half and leaned back through to kiss me squarely on the mouth.

"Did you know this is called a Dutch door?" I said. We both started to laugh.

"I know you have apple cheeks," he said, giving me another kiss before he ran across the lawn and disappeared into the house. The kettle began to sing, and I thought its sound the nicest in the whole world.

After our tea, we went out to the living room, where I sank into the deep velvet sofa, and Johannes brought out his violin. He fussed with the strings and played a few notes and then fussed some more. Eventually, a melancholy but beautiful melody filled the room, and the music seemed to float out through the windows, where it drifted in the air like leaves. I wondered if he was hoping to play out all the sorrow he was holding inside.

I remembered the time Grandma had taken me to a student concert at Whitman College in Walla Walla. The music that summer night was magical. Grandma said it was from "Appalachian Spring" by Aaron Copland. I wanted to get up and dance or sing. I had to hold onto my chair to keep from jumping up and moving to the sounds that spilled out into the room. This time was different. It felt like church, like I mustn't move until the music stopped.

"How did you learn to play like that?" I asked, clapping

like crazy. "That was wonderful, like listening to a concert on the radio, even better."

Johannes face reddened. "My mother was my teacher. She . . . " But he didn't get to finish.

"*Hallo*!" came from both the hall and the kitchen. Elisabeth was home from her lesson, and Tante Dee was back in the kitchen. The aroma of curry and other spices I couldn't recognize soon brought us in to join her.

"Tante is preparing *rijsttafel* for you tonight. You will like," said Elisabeth.

"It is 'rice table' in English," said Johannes. "Many dishes to choose from. Some are, how do you say . . . spicy and will bite your tongue. I will help you choose."

I helped Elisabeth set the table, and watched her handle each one of the blue and white plates tenderly. "Delftware," she said. "They are the only treasures Tante was able to bring from home." She held up a plate. "They are lovely, no?" She clutched one to her chest, and her face lit up. I'd never thought about dishes as treasures, but then I'd never had to leave my entire life behind.

When we had put out the last of the silverware and the napkins, Elisabeth took my hand. "I have never seen Jon with such a crush." She gave me a funny little crooked smile. "Such a silly word to speak of love."

All through dinner, Johannes kept reaching under the table

to grab my hand, aware the whole time that his sister knew what he was doing. She kept looking at us, trying hard not to laugh. Finally, she tried to smother a giggle by coughing into her napkin. Her aunt turned and whispered to her.

Elisabeth looked down at her plate, but I could see the corners of her mouth twitching. All at once, everyone around the table burst out laughing. Johannes cheeks flushed.

"Tante," he said, drawing in a deep breath. "Tonight's curry is much seasoned." He took a big gulp of water. I could tell by their wide smiles no one was fooled. Johannes grabbed my hand again and gave it a squeeze. I smiled back, but those big smiles had already begun to fade. Even when we laughed, there was still sadness in this house.

Chapter 13

Elisabeth and I were left to wash up the dishes while Tante Dee went to the main house to tidy the kitchen and turn down the beds. I figured Uncle Hendrik was trying to keep his nephew busy because he sent Johannes for the cards and challenged him to a game.

"It is *Pandoeren*, a game from home," said Elisabeth. "Uncle's favorite. It is not to my liking. Cards," she sighed. "I'd rather draw or practice my violin."

When the special dishes were all carefully washed and dried and put away, we went to sit in the little nook by the windows. I wanted to tell her about my drawing lessons with Miss Moore and the funny piano teacher I'd had in Seattle, the one with the walrus mustache and the creepy house that smelled of mothballs and vinegar. I didn't want to admit to her that I'd absolutely hated those lessons and finally, Mama let me quit.

When a funny little buzzer sounded two short bursts,

Uncle Hendrik hurried through the kitchen, said something to Elisabeth, and flew out the back door. "That was from the main house," she said. "I must go with Uncle to see what is needed."

Johannes stuck his head in the kitchen. He had my coat in his hand. "Annie, let's walk."

I couldn't imagine what we could see in the dark, but once outside, I could only stare in wonder. The endless rolling lawn glowed with garden lights and millions of fairy lamps hung from trees and arbors. A few spring crocuses were just beginning to peek out in the flower beds. At one end of the grounds, a tennis court was ablaze with flood lights. I could just hear Mama: "Their electric bill must be the size of the national debt." But to me it was like stumbling into a storybook paradise.

When we got to the greenhouse, Johannes pulled me down next to him on an old wicker sofa. For a long time we just sat silently, our shoulders touching. I had never sat so close to a boy all alone, but I didn't want to move. Every so often, Johannes shifted. Clearly, he had something on his mind, but he said nothing.

When he suddenly stood up, I thought he was ready to go back to the cottage. "Annie, I need to tell you something of myself. I do not see your eyes until I tell to you my story." Johannes looked down at his feet. "My mama and papa are both dead — at home — from war. Perhaps you know already."

I couldn't think what to say. My brain wouldn't budge.

"At first," said Johannes, "when the Nazis come, Mama and Papa aren't worried. Soldiers sometimes gave us sweets and sausage. But later, everything changed."

Johannes continued to study something on his shoe. "Do you know of the Dutch Resistance?"

"I know about the French Resistance." I whispered. My grade school friends and I had played at being Resistance fighters. We played that game endlessly, traveling in packs from yard to yard. My stomach tightened. I was sure what Johannes was about to tell me was not about children's games.

"My cousin Herman was part of the movement, and once in a while I sneak from my house in early morning and help him while he and his friends lay in wait for trains bringing German soldiers. No one questioned a boy with only his skates over his shoulder."

Johannes paused and let out a deep sigh. "I see my cousin last when we are hiding in an abandoned windmill. Our morning has been a success. Two German train cars destroyed. He finally decides it is safe for me to run home. Herman finds an old *zeis* — a blade for cutting grain — and makes me take it."

I suddenly had to take in a surprised gulp of air. I hadn't realized that for the last few moments I'd been holding my breath. Johannes came over and reached for my hand, and we went to stand in the doorway, our fingers touching, watching the night sky.

"When Herman does not return home," he began again, "we can only hope he is still hiding and will soon be smuggled out of Holland. For days Mama and her sister Greet wait for news. It is too dangerous to pass messages. We hear nothing."

I felt his body stiffen, and he turned away from me. "Mama and Papa, Elisabeth and I plan to celebrate our tenth birthday. We have no cake. We haven't eaten anything but beetroot and maybe a potato for weeks. It is winter, and we know great hunger, and Papa has warned we will have nothing but tulip bulbs if the Allies don't reach us soon. Mama has told me to take Elisabeth to our barn to play. I think it strange. It is our special day, and I am waiting to see what Papa has planned for us, but Mama says we stay in our barn until she or Papa comes for us. I yell at her. I don't want to go. I think I am too big to be treated like a little child. She hands me Papa's camera and tells me it is my present and points to door. I am so angry I yank Elisabeth's arm and pull her outside."

Johannes's eyes had turned vacant and his face had this flat look, like he was sleepwalking. Did it hurt too much for him to go on? I wondered if I should leave or go look for Uncle Hendrik.

Finally Johannes sat back down on the old sofa, and I sat beside him. He seemed calmer. He whispered, "I knew something was wrong, but I yelled at Mama. I yelled. She must have been frightened, but I didn't understand." He bent over, resting his elbows on his knees and pressing his face into his hands. "Mama was sending me away," he said softly. His voice had become hoarse and low-pitched. "I remember looking back toward our house, tears streaming down my face, my hands making fists. She was standing at kitchen window smiling and waving."

I reached for Johannes's hand, and his grip was so strong, my hand began to tingle. His story was not over.

"Elisabeth is restless and hungry. I try to stop her, but she runs out of our barn and starts across the field. I hear the rumble of motorcycles — German soldiers — and know I should go after her, but I am afraid for Mama, too. When I hear shots, I run back to the house. A sound of heavy boots echoes above my head. Cupboard doors are slamming and men laughing."

All at once Johannes leaped up and bolted across the mossy dirt floor, pushing a row of flowerpots off a shelf with one hand. I flinched at the sound of pottery breaking all around me. "Johannes, you're scaring me."

He sat back down and reached for my hand, weaving my fingers into his. Despite the cold, his hands were warm and moist. "Papa is on floor in pantry. Mama is beside him. Her arm is across his chest, maybe listening to his heart. It is not so. Both are dead."

"Oh no!" My throat felt heavy, like I'd swallowed wet sand.

"I run toward our barn; I had to find Elisabeth and get us safely to Tante Greet's, but I think — soldiers will be there, too. It is Herman they are after. A soldier comes out holding a pistol. He turns and shouts to his comrade. Elisabeth has stopped halfway across the field and is running back toward our barn. The soldier starts toward her." Johannes's jaw had tightened, and his voice was hard and flat. "He doesn't expect me; I pick up my blade and swing it, catching him across his throat from behind. We struggle." Johannes stopped to take in a big breath, rubbing at the scar on his arm. "The soldier, he drops his pistol. I shoot him — with his own gun. I wait for the other soldier to leave the house. I see he is just a boy, like me. I kill him, too."

The tears had dried on Johannes's face, but suddenly he slumped forward, curling himself into a ball. He rocked back and forth, letting out short, high-pitched cries. It was the same sound my rabbit made the night he died, and I learned that rabbits can howl, but only when they are in pain.

"My last words to Mama were angry ones," Johannes sobbed. "I see her eyes still and will never forgive myself."

Johannes reached over and touched my cheek. "Can you care for me, such a person?"

Just when I thought I could finally breathe again, my stomach twisted into knots. I had no answer. I was numb.

Chapter 14

Elisabeth wanted to ride back with me when Uncle Hendrik said it was time to leave. She had come looking for us, and I wondered if she realized what had happened, maybe even heard Johannes. On the way to my house, we sat together in the back seat and she held my hand tightly in hers.

She didn't let go until I stepped out of the car. "Annie, thank you. You are our friend. It means so much."

I could only smile and squeeze her hand goodbye. Staggering into the living room, I could feel my head spinning with Johannes's story. My whole body down to my fingertips was reeling. All mashed together were memories of Uncle Billy the year I lived with Grandma Hattie when he'd come home from the war with his head full of ghosts. I also couldn't help but think of the day of our bike ride and Johannes's reaction to the boys who picked on him. And Daddy and Mama — they still hadn't been able to shorten the distance the war had put between them. All that hurt. All that anger. If my head had any room left for a headache, it was going to be a dilly.

Daddy and Uncle Billy were in the living room, huddled next to the radio, listening to *Truth or Consequences*, Daddy's favorite show. It was a silly program, but when the contestants got really crazy consequences for their wrong answers, it was a scream. That kind of silliness wasn't what I needed at the moment, so I didn't stick around. I found Mama and Grandma Hattie in the kitchen. It was clear they were having a real serious conversation. From the tones in their voices and their fake smiles, I figured they might be talking about me. Just my luck. A headache was definitely a possibility.

"It's almost nine o'clock," said Mama. "We were just about to call the VanderVeldes and send your grandmother over to pick you up."

Great! Mama was in the mood for one of her discussions. Her mouth had that sour-pickle look that signaled she was going to lay down a new set of house rules. Grandma let out a small sigh. She was letting me know the "we" did not include her.

"Your grandmother tells me the VanderVeldes are nice people, but I haven't met them yet. Your father seems to feel the uncle is a decent sort, but then, he trusts everyone. And your grandmother has just told me that your special friend Johannes is sixteen." Mama paused and took a sip of her coffee. "Even if he is in your class, sixteen is too old for you."

I looked at Grandma and mouthed "sixteen?" and she gave me a little nod.

Mama was too busy concentrating on announcing her rules and didn't notice our exchange. "I think for the time being you'd better see this boy only at school. We'll talk more about this tomorrow."

"Sure. OK, Mama."

Having made herself clear with no backtalk from me, Mama swept out of the kitchen doing her best queen bee imitation.

"C'mon, Sweetpea," said Grandma with a wink, "where's that Annie Leigh Howard spunk? I expected at least a squeak out of you."

"I don't have one bit of spunk left in my whole body, Grandma."

"My, my! That sounds serious."

"Johannes talked about the war."

"Ah, I see." Grandma got up and filled a jelly glass with water. "That is truly serious. Do you want to tell me about it?"

"Not now, Grandma. Maybe tomorrow."

"Of course. In the meantime, help me finish the puzzle I've set up on a card table next to the piano. Matching the pieces is giving me fits. I have half a mind to get out my nail file and shave a few edges." Grandma poured herself another glass of water and took two big gulps. "I must say, talking to your mama is thirsty work. I thought she was going to send me home because I'd let you go to the VanderVeldes' house." Finally, an honest-to-goodness Grandma smile. "You don't really have to work on the puzzle, but I would like it if you'd come to church with me tomorrow." She dabbed at her mouth with the edge of her apron. "I'd like to visit that Baptist church over on Sixth. After the service we could find one of those root beer places, order a float, and you and I could have one of our nice long talks."

But we didn't get to church the next morning. We'd gotten ourselves all dressed up in our Sunday best only to have Grandma's old Ford sputter out about two gasps and then give up altogether. Before we could borrow the pickup, Billy left to check on some special rosewood. Grandma had to make do with the radio preacher, which she didn't much enjoy. "Land sakes," she sighed, "if I wanted to listen to fire and brimstone, I could go to a Walla Walla city council meeting."

When Billy got back, he made Grandma an offer. "Ma, my apartment could sure use a good scrub down. In exchange, I'll take your car to a buddy of mine tomorrow who'll fix it up just fine."

"I wonder who gets the best out of that deal?" said Grandma. "Hardly seems a fair exchange."

"I'll help," I offered. It would be easier for Grandma Hattie, and I'd have her all to myself. She'd sort out what was bothering me, but she'd need a lot more than a nail file.

The next morning we lugged about a year's worth of Billy's clothes to the wobbly washer in the garage. Grandma and I wrestled with the wringer, and I wondered if Mama would ever get a new washing machine, one that didn't leave me feeling like I'd spent the afternoon playing tug-of-war. Since the sky hinted at rain, we had to haul the whole mess to the basement to dry on the indoor line.

"Grandma," I said, taking a clothespin out of my mouth, "why didn't you tell me Johannes was sixteen?"

"I figured you knew. And it isn't like you two are going to elope or something. Plus I like the VanderVeldes a lot." Grandma finished hanging the last pair of Billy's socks on the line and put her hands on her hips for emphasis. "Land sakes, your mama has no idea how much they've all been through. Why, it's more than a body should have to endure. Those two kids — they need to feel welcomed and cared for."

I wondered just how much my sweet grandma knew about what Elisabeth and Johannes had endured. When we were back in Billy's apartment changing the sheets, and no one could hear us, I told her most of the story I'd heard the day before, leaving out some of the details about pistols and dead soldiers.

"I knew most of that," said Grandma, snapping the top sheet with a sharp crack before she let it fall on the bed. "That day we were there for tea, Dee confided in me and shared how worried she's been about the two of them. And not just because they ended up in classes with younger kids. I think she feels relieved that they are both fairly healthy, considering they'd been scared half to death all of their young lives, eating sugar beets and tulip bulbs just to stay alive. She's awfully pleased they've made a friend like you."

It occurred to me that Auntie Dee might not be too pleased if she also knew about the kissing. As for Mama's reaction, it didn't bear thinking about.

How much did the VanderVeldes even understand about Johannes and the day his parents died? At the moment, I didn't even understand how I felt about all I knew.

"Mama's probably right, Grandma. I should spend less time at the VanderVeldes' and more time with Miss Moore. She has her heart set on me entering work in that all-city exhibit. I've barely started working in watercolor. Anyway, Elisabeth and I can see each other at school, and Johannes and I have a class together."

I wasn't sure when I'd talk to Johannes. My mind kept going back to Uncle Billy and that summer at Grandma's when I saw firsthand what the war had done to him. All these invisible wounds had pierced his soul something fierce.

When I got to social studies class on Monday, Johannes's seat was empty, and it stayed that way the whole hour.

Mr. Raymond was absent, too. For once the room didn't reek of peanuts and stale cigar smoke. Our sub reminded me of a large rabbit, his nose twitching the whole time he rambled on, warning us that the Russians were planning to land in Commencement Bay at any moment. For some reason that possibility struck some of the boys as funny. I mean, it was like Mr. Raymond had left a script. After struggling to smother their laughter, the Hamilton twins could no longer hold it in. The sub knew he was doomed.

When we were let out early for lunch, the whole class burst through the door in a whoop of giggles. I suppose I should have been worried about Russian bombs — the papers were still full of all kinds of frightful stuff. But it seemed to me there were poor souls around me who had demons a whole lot scarier than those old Russians.

Chapter 15

I was glad to see Elisabeth waiting for me outside the cafeteria. We took our lunches to the farthest corner. I didn't particularly want to be near the "popular girls." They had names like Grace and Melody, but they weren't one bit graceful or agreeable sounding. I'd heard the laughter and the ugly remarks they made about Elisabeth, calling her Heidi because of her braids and mimicking her accent. She was as pretty as the skating star Sonja Henie, who had an accent and braids. No one made fun of her.

Elisabeth unwrapped a chicken salad sandwich on homemade bread. She handed me half. "Uncle Hendrik took Jon with him this morning. They go to Canada to see some relatives." She let out a deep sigh. "There is too much sadness at our house."

I took a big bite of chicken salad and was tempted to gobble the rest. The sandwich was heavenly. Elisabeth took tiny bites and chewed for several minutes. She and Johannes were the slowest eaters I'd ever seen. But I guess I would be, too, if I'd had to chew on an old beet, or worse, a bitter tulip bulb, and make it last through breakfast, lunch, and dinner.

"Why don't you come home with me today?" I asked, knowing full well that it was Mama's day off, so she might be less than pleased. But I could count on Grandma to smooth things over.

Elisabeth beamed. "I would like that very much, Annie. I call Tante Dee after school."

We fell into an easygoing pattern after that. Lunch at school together every noon and art lessons twice a week with Miss Moore. I didn't have to beg Miss Moore one bit to let Elisabeth join us. For the first time I had a real best friend close to my own age. Of course, Miss Gloria had been my closest friend the year I lived at Grandma's, but she was more like a big sister. Elisabeth was the real thing. We both laughed at radio shows like *You Bet Your Life* with Groucho Marx. We told each other secrets and got silly together. She taught me how to skate in circles. I was teaching her how to jitterbug.

Johannes had been away for three weeks. I wondered how Uncle Hendrik could stay away from his job for such a long time. Elisabeth was particularly quiet about anything to do with Johannes. She must have known about what happened that evening and understood I was still working through what he'd told me. I knew men killed in war, but what about boys killing boys? He'd saved Elisabeth's life, but what did it feel like to look someone square in the eye and pull the trigger? I shuddered thinking about it.

Uncle Billy had come home with that war stuck so tight in his head that he just about lost his mind. It was hard to know what was going on with Johannes, even when I saw only his sweet side. Spending so much time with him and then having to sort through everything that had happened, I'd barely had space in my brain for anything else. I'd even gotten sidetracked and not had my talk with Daddy, and had only recently realized I'd been taking Grandma for granted. She'd already stayed longer than usual, partially for me. Then one morning she announced she was going back to Walla Walla.

"You know, Sweetpea," she said, handing me a stack of pancakes, "I've been here quite a spell; I can't stay here forever. Running a grocery store is what I do best. I'm not the best choice for chief cook and bottle washer."

"I wish you didn't live so far away. You could visit every weekend." Having Grandma Hattie around had warmed up the house considerably.

"That would be a treat, but what about your young man and that lovely Elisabeth? Your mama is bound to let you go back to the VanderVeldes' house. A little bird tells me that Hendrik and Jon will be back by the weekend. Three weeks should have given your mama time to cool down."

"It's all right, Grandma. I've got so much to do. I haven't thought about Johannes much," I lied.

"Hmmm! Uh-huh! So, absence didn't make your heart grow fonder? Or is that nose of yours about an inch longer than usual?"

"I don't know, Grandma, really, but I'll figure it out. But you can't go until you help me talk to Daddy. At least about getting a guide dog. I know he'll be happier once he sees the difference it will make."

"Billy and I have done a little digging. There's still that fellow from the convalescent hospital who got in touch with your daddy about that veterans' organization. Billy and I both talked to your mama, but we need more details about what's available before we start moving mountains." Grandma gave one of her crooked smiles. "I didn't bring up anything specifically about guide dogs with your mama, just that we were looking into resources for your daddy. Anyway, Billy is going to write that fellow and see if he would get in touch again." Grandma slid another stack of pancakes onto my plate, put the griddle back on the stove, and sat down across from me. She took her time pouring herself a cup of coffee. "You know, for a guide dog or any additional rehabilitation he might have to go away for awhile. Are you sure that's what you want?"

"How far away? Surely not miles and miles. Anyway, if

that's the case, I'll just go with him."

Grandma took a swallow of her coffee and shrugged, "Don't get your hopes up, Sweetpea. It might mean more changes than you or your mama can make easily. Plus, your dad can be stubborn."

"I know, but surely he wants to be more independent." Of course, in my excitement about helping Daddy, I had no idea what I was asking of all of us.

Grandma reached across the table and gave my cheek a good pinch. "If anyone can convince him, it's you, not me. You're just as stubborn sometimes as he is."

"Ouch, Gram! You haven't pinched my cheek since I was five."

"I figure I need to do it once in a while, just to keep my hand in. Grandma privilege."

I poured the last of the coffee into Grandma's cup. "I've been meaning to tell you about the other day. When I ran over to Wolfe's for butter, a man came into the store with a big German shepherd leading him, and when I left, the man and his dog came out right after me, and we got to the corner just as the bus was taking off, and that dog waited until it was safe to cross and off they went." I was talking so fast my throat got all scratchy, so I took a quick sip of Grandma's coffee and then kept going. "I figure Daddy should at least look into having a dog. Think how much more he could do on his own. If he can't get his sight back, maybe he can at least do more of the things he did before the war."

"Whoa, Annie. Slow down. One thing at a time. You can't just rush into making all kinds of plans on your own, no matter how much you want to. Yes, you have your daddy's well-being at heart, but he has to make the final decisions. Don't push too hard. A guide dog is a wonderful idea, and we all want to help, but in the end your daddy is the one who decides, who makes the effort. We can't hand him back his independence. He has to find his own way."

Grandma stood up and smoothed out her apron. "Come here, Sweetpea. You're not too big to give your old granny a hug." She held out her arms, and I slipped into that big comfort circle. "Now, sweetie," she whispered into my ear, "one of these days you have to tell me what else is rolling around in that whirligig mind of yours."

Chapter 16

Grandma knew me too well. It was hard not to just grab her arm and say, "Don't go. I need to tell you . . ." And then spill the beans about Gardenia Man and Johannes and the German soldiers and how important it was to talk to Mama, not just Daddy, about how everything didn't feel peachy keen.

Turned out my wish came true, only in a mean kind of way. On Saturday, the very first day of April, right after dinner, Grandma took a tumble on the back steps and broke her wrist. There was no way she could drive all the way back to Walla Walla. I knew she must be in pain, but I had to admit that part of me was secretly pleased she couldn't go home for a while. To make up for being a two-faced ninny, I promised myself to wait on her hand and foot.

Dr. Miller came to the house immediately and took care of her with his usual stern but kindly bedside manner. I wondered if anyone else noticed how much he looked like one of the Smith Brothers on the cough drop box. He even lingered for coffee and some lemon sponge cake with Daddy and Uncle Billy. I followed Grandma back to the sewing room, her bedroom for a few days longer.

"April Fools, indeed! I'm going to be absolutely useless until the cast comes off," Grandma sighed. "Dang it all! What a nasty turn of events. Gloria and Will can manage, but I shouldn't stay away so long."

I got her my old radio so she could listen to her favorite shows in peace and quiet. It was already enough that she had to share her room with Mama's crumbling dressmaker form, a creepy headless, legless body on a wire frame. Not to mention piles of old, faded fabric and jars of buttons and stacks of tattered patterns that were forever slipping off their shelves. Grandma didn't like to be fussed over and rarely complained, but I intended to make her as snug and comfortable as possible. I'd just gotten a set of clean sheets from the linen closet and was about to change her bed when we heard loud, angry voices coming from the kitchen.

Grandma's eyes narrowed, and she put her finger to her lips. I went to the doorway and listened.

"It's Mama and Daddy." I couldn't make out the words, and I expect Grandma couldn't either. Just voices yelling over each other, rising and falling, sharp and fierce like that January blizzard screaming through the trees. I'd overheard their "discussions" plenty of times, but this was different. Mama's bad moods usually meant she got tight-lipped and gave us the silent treatment for a while. "What should we do, Grandma?"

"My land, child," she said, sitting down on the bed with a deep sigh. "Lordy, I swear. I don't know."

A loud bang signaled the back door had slammed shut. Most likely Daddy heading for the workshop. I hoped Dr. Miller had long gone. But where was Uncle Billy?

"Sweetpea, you'd best reconnoiter. See if the fireworks are over." Grandma lay back and sank into her pillows. "Cowardly of me, I know, but I'm not up to any more drama tonight. Leave the bed. We can change it tomorrow."

It wasn't like Grandma to hand over her role as family mediator, but I figured she was worn to a frazzle. She waved me off, and I went out to the kitchen. Not a soul, but I thought I heard Mama on the phone. I tiptoed out the back and out to the workshop.

"Daddy, it's me," I said, switching on the light. "What's going on?"

He was sitting at the worktable, the radio playing Glenn Miller in the background. He was turning something shiny over and over in the palm of his hand, the muscles in his jaw pulled taut. "I ever tell you about my first glimpse of the English Coast? Those great massive cliffs of Dover." He went quiet for a minute, opening and closing his hand. I got a quick glimpse and realized he was holding his pilot's wings. "Flying over the countryside," he continued, "the land laid out like a patchwork quilt all in a million shades of green. Took my breath away. A fighter pilot, alone in the cockpit, has his own special kind of freedom. Kind of like the first time you ride a bike with no hands. I never felt that free before."

I wasn't exactly sure what had happened between Mama and Daddy, but it seemed best to just stay put and listen.

"And those P-51 Mustangs. Flying low over the fields. Dang, what a rush!" Daddy turned those wings over and over in his hand. "Those machines could really show a fellow what he's made of. Made you more aware of your limits, too." All this time he'd been talking into the worktable and the wings in his hand, but he turned and reached out, motioning me to come close. I stepped into his outstretched arm and leaned in against him. "Open your hand, Annie Leigh." I did as I was told, and Daddy placed the wings against my palm, the metal warm and moist from all those turns in his hand. "These are for you, my girl." He closed his fingers over mine and squeezed my hand. I felt the pin stick one of my fingers. Like a bee sting. But I didn't make a peep.

I looked over at Daddy and studied his face. His jaw had re-laxed, and the lines in his face gone smooth. He seemed a million miles away, lost in the clouds, most likely getting ready to make another low pass over those amazing white cliffs of Dover.

Chapter 17

Uncle Billy met me at the back door. "What's going on? Where is everybody? Ma's in her room with the door closed, and your mom just flew out the front door like a bat outta hell." He seemed really and truly confused, and I wondered where he'd been when the fireworks started.

Just like Uncle Billy to be absolutely without a clue. "Didn't you hear them? Mama and Daddy had a humdinger of an argument. Grandma's probably playing it safe and staying in her room to avoid the fallout."

"Not like Ma. She usually has to put in her two cents worth, but then, that broken wrist has probably slowed her down." Billy took out his pocket watch. "It's getting late. Your dad out in the workshop?"

"Yep, but I think you probably need to leave him be for a while."

"That bad, huh? I was out talking to the doc. Talking about

your dad, as a matter of fact."

"Where'd Mama go?" I felt a flutter in my stomach. The possibility of Gardenia Man having anything to do with any of this made me ready to puke.

"I heard her on the phone. Could be wrong, but sounded like she was calling a taxi." Uncle Billy stood there scratching his head. "Looks like you and me are on kitchen duty tonight. Dinner's not going to fix itself."

Billy ended up scrambling eggs, and I made buttermilk biscuits. Since Grandma had most likely decided to stay put in her room, I took a plate into her.

"Good heavens, Sweetpea, what time is it? I must have dozed off." Grandma sat up with some difficulty, pushing herself up with her good hand.

"It's after six. I brought us some dinner," I said, placing her plate carefully on the nightstand and mine on the extra chair. "Billy did the eggs. The lopsided biscuits are my contribution."

"A lopsided biscuit is scarcely a tragedy anytime, but considering today's events, it hardly bears mentioning." Grandma let out a big sigh. "Any news from the battlefront?"

"Billy thinks Mama took a taxi somewhere, and Daddy's out in the workshop." I pulled the chair over to use as my table and stretched out next to Grandma on the bed.

"A taxi? What's got into Dorothy? It's not like her to go gallivanting. Maybe she called a friend to pick her up. Probably needed a little time to cool off." Grandma put down her plate and gave another deep sigh.

Grandma would have washed my mouth out with soap if I'd told her what I really thought Mama was doing. Other folks could act crazy and as plain ornery as they wanted. For the time being, until the armistice, I planned to stay where I was, safe in Grandma Hattie territory.

Much later I woke up to the sound of dance music and muffled voices out in the living room. I was ice cold and had a nasty crick in my neck. I'd fallen asleep, sitting straight up against the headboard. Grandma was snoring in little whoops next to me. I got off the bed as quietly as I could and crept out to see what in the world was going on.

I got as far as the dining room and realized it was Mama and Daddy. They were dancing, ever so slowly, to the music on the phonograph. Mama had her head against Daddy's shoulder, and he was singing along with the Harry James orchestra, "I don't want to walk without you, ba-by / Walk without my arms about you, ba-by." The music warmed me in a way no cup of hot chocolate ever could.

I hadn't heard Daddy sing in a long time. People always told him he had a voice as easy on the ear as Bing Crosby's. It was hard to stay upset listening to Daddy sound so sweet. I lingered a while and then tiptoed back to my room and went to bed, smiling to myself. Daddy singing. That was definitely a good sign.

All that sweetness didn't keep everyone from walking on eggshells for days on end. Several times I thought I would talk to Daddy, maybe bring up the idea of a guide dog. Somehow the time never seemed right, and I was grateful for the calm.

One afternoon after school, alone with Elisabeth in my room, I decided to ask her plain and simple why Johannes had been gone so long. She'd been teaching me how to knit. All the girls were making argyle socks for their boyfriends. It was all the rage, and I decided Johannes deserved a pair as much as any other boy at school.

"Please tell me. Where's your brother?" I put down my knitting, the bobbins clicking like castanets, and looked her straight in the eye. "The truth, please."

Elisabeth quickly looked away and held up my sorry attempt at knitting socks. "I think maybe you stick to mittens."

"C'mon, I know something is wrong."

"Uncle took him to see some people from home. Maybe his friends help Jon." Elisabeth could only stare at the rag rug on the floor and shake her head. "I promise not to say anything."

"What kind of help? What's so wrong I can't know about it?"

"Jon has had a very bad time. His nights are full of terrible dreams." Elisabeth fidgeted and played with the yarn. "I tell you too much."

"It's the war, isn't it? It's that awful war in his head."

"Tante and Uncle try to help, but Jon cannot let go of what happened at home. He gets into fights." Elisabeth lowered her voice and breathed in slowly. "Uncle was afraid Jon was, how you say, falling apart, and we wouldn't be able to hold him together. So they go — for help."

I went numb. So that was it. Just like Uncle Billy. Johannes couldn't let go of the war.

"I'm glad you told me, Elisabeth." I reached out and took her hand. She squeezed it and then brushed away the tears sliding down her cheeks.

"Let's go play music," she said. "If I have Chopin, I don't fall apart."

We had just opened up the piano and chosen some sheet music when the doorbell rang.

Out on the doorstep was a tall man in dark glasses and a big old grin. A mass of curls stuck out in little red springs all over his head. He was holding onto a large German shepherd. I opened the door a crack.

"Hello there," he said, sticking out his hand. "I'm looking for Eddie Howard. I'm Rory Lee Murphy, and this here is Montgomery. Who might I be speaking to?"

"I'm Annie Howard," I said, opening the door wider and taking his hand. "Eddie's daughter."

"Well, I guess I found the right place then." And with that

he and his dog Montgomery stepped right into the front hall. "That's a mighty firm grip, Miss Annie Howard," he said with a chuckle. "You're Eddie's daughter, all right."

Chapter 18

I offered Mr. Murphy my arm and guided him into the living room and over to the wing chair. "I'll go get Daddy. My friend Elisabeth is here. If you need anything, just let her know." Mr. Murphy gave a funny little salute and pretended to click his heels.

I didn't have to go far. Daddy had just come into the kitchen, having heard a car pull up in front. "We have visitors?" he said, giving his hands a good wash at the sink. "Are they just sitting out there on their own?"

"Don't worry, Daddy. Elisabeth is with him."

"Him? Him who?" Daddy gave me a curious, lopsided look. I hoped I hadn't made a mistake and let some stranger into our house.

"It's a Mr. Rory Lee Murphy. He says he knows you." Daddy followed me out to the living room where Elisabeth was standing at the side window describing to our visitor the

Hinkles' house and the raggedy cats and Ella Mae, who was sneaking in and out of our azaleas, pretending to be looking for something.

"Spud? Spud Murphy is right here in my living room?" Daddy let go of me and stepped forward, reaching out his hand. "Spud, you old devil, is that you?"

Montgomery gave a low whine. "It's OK, boy." Mr. Murphy gave him a pat. "My dog just wants to make sure you're friendly." Moving in the direction of Daddy's voice, he clasped Daddy's outstretched hand. "Eddie, you old rascal! It's been too long. Been waitin' to hear from you. Not a word. Not even a postcard! Took me a spell to work out where y'all got to."

Daddy grabbed Mr. Murphy's shoulder. "Now, Annie Leigh, I guess you and Elisabeth already met this young fellow from Texas. Galveston, if I remember correctly. But let me tell you, he's the only Irishman with a drawl I ever met. What's more — that's no brogue. Why, that twang could take the enamel right off your teeth. And you don't need to tell me the color of his hair. 'Cause it's so red, even a blind man can see it. " Daddy gave Mr. Murphy a couple of thumps on the back. "Sit down, sit down. What are you up to these days, Spud?" I steered Daddy over to the sofa.

Mr. Spud, with a little help from Elisabeth, moved over to the wing chair and eased himself down. Montgomery immediately went to sit down beside him.

"Well, Eddie, I came to see you. That's what. See what you've been up to. Wanted to make sure my old buddy wasn't just sittin' on his backside doing nothing." Mr. Murphy emphasized this last part with a few taps on the arm of the chair. "Thought maybe I could interest you in helping out some of the fellas we both know from Old Farms Convalescent Hospital."

"Well now, Spud, I'm not one to sit around just waiting for my army check. My brother and I've started our own carpentry business. We expect to do real well." Daddy's voice trembled a little on the last part, and I wondered if he actually worried things wouldn't go well at all.

"Now, Annie, you might get us something to drink and a plate of those cookies your mama brought home yesterday."

"Nothing to eat for me, thank you kindly, but a glass of something cold would be real welcome." Spud Murphy shifted in his chair and leaned forward. Montgomery stirred. "Eddie, I was hoping I could recruit you to work with us in the Blinded Veterans Association. We could use some help. You know, reaching out to some of the guys out here."

I knew I should be on my way into the kitchen, but I sure wasn't about to leave the room until I heard what Daddy had to say.

"Well, Spud, I have a lot of responsibility here with the family and all, and just getting the business started. Not sure what help I'd be." That tremor was in Daddy's voice again, a sure signal he was not comfortable with being asked to help.

Seemed to me this Spud Murphy, with his fire-engine red hair and big dog, was what Grandma would call "just the ticket" to get Daddy out on his own. All sorts of ideas were dancing around in my head. A whole conga line was about to bust through.

"Annie Leigh, what about those cookies? And I think there's some cider in the cold pantry."

That was Daddy's "I mean business" voice, so I got up, and Elisabeth followed me into the kitchen, where she helped me fix a tray of cookies and pour mugs of cider.

"That Mr. Spud person. He is very handsome, yes?" said Elisabeth. A big grin spread into a blush across her face. "Such a funny way he sings his words."

"Elisabeth VanderVelde! You are *too much*. He's way too old. Why, for heaven's sakes, he's got to be at least twenty-five." Then I started to giggle. "But he is cute, isn't he?"

Once back in the living room, we played at being hostess and passed around the cookies and topped up the mugs with more cider. I noticed Mr. Spud took two cookies and gave one to Montgomery. Elisabeth turned red all over again when Mr. Spud asked where she was from and in that drawl of his went on about how she had such a lovely speaking voice, he bet she must sing a "mean" song. Later I had to explain that a "mean" song wasn't what he meant literally. Daddy had taken a couple of cookies but had left them untouched on the end table. The mood in the room had definitely changed while we were out in the kitchen.

Uncle Billy came in from the workshop to see what had kept Daddy, and then Grandma joined us. After hearing all the activity in the living room, she wasn't about to be left out. Daddy made all the introductions, but the tone in his voice was certainly cooler.

What was it about Spud Murphy from Texas that had put Daddy on edge?

I mean, I'd been hoping to find a way to get Daddy in touch with someone who could help, and here he was. And with a guide dog as well!

"Well, Spud," said Daddy, "I don't expect you drove here on your own. Some poor private sitting out there all this time, waiting to drive you back to wherever?"

"Matter of fact, there is, so I best be going." He reached out for Daddy's hand once more. "Think about what I said, Eddie. I don't intend to take no for an answer." He moved around the room shaking hands with everyone, holding Elisabeth's hand the longest, causing her to blush all the way to the roots of her hair. "I expect to see y'all real soon; you can plan on it. Now maybe your daughter could walk me out to my car."

I gave Elisabeth a look, but she shook her head. I was on

my own. So Mr. Spud, Montgomery, and I walked out to the official-looking army car parked at the edge of the curb. The driver leapt out and immediately snapped to attention. Then he hurried to open the car doors. His uniform ballooned out around him, like it was intended for a man much taller and wider. He didn't look old enough to drive, let alone be in the army. Mr. Murphy felt for the car door, but before he got in, he turned in my direction. Montgomery had already hopped right into the back seat.

"Annie Leigh Howard," Mr. Murphy said, stepping forward to shake my hand again. "I bet there isn't anything you can't make happen once you put your mind to it. I'd be real pleased if you could get your daddy to think about being part of our organization."

I wondered if I could. Grandma had said only Daddy could make the decision to be more independent. But . . . maybe I could give him a little push.

"Tell you what, Mr. Murphy. You help me get Daddy a dog for himself. Then maybe together we can get him to work with you and those other fellows."

"There it is, young lady. There's that Howard spunk I know so well! When we were in the hospital together, your dad was hell on wheels. Wouldn't let any of us feel sorry for ourselves. He needs to get that determination, that gumption back."

"I've been trying for ages to get an adult to listen to me

about Daddy. I hoped it would be Grandma or Uncle Billy who would get the ball rolling, but you'll have to do." I hoped I didn't sound like a smart-aleck, but here was my chance and I wasn't going to lose it. "So where do I begin?"

"Getting a dog is a start, young lady. That would be a fine beginning." He waved over his driver. "Private, take one of my cards and write this number down on the back." The two of them walked over to the hood of the car and the soldier wrote down what Mr. Murphy told him.

"Now, Miss Annie, this is a number where you can find out how to help your daddy apply for a dog. My number's printed on the other side if you need my help." He reached out, and I shook his hand again. "That's what men do, little lady, settle a deal with a handshake. I'd be proud to shake your hand any day of the week."

It was a new experience being spoken to like an adult, and I didn't want Mr. Spud to think I was a silly kid. "Thank you for visiting today, sir. It means a lot."

"Sir! Golly, that makes me feel as old as the hills. Call me Spud. Everyone does." He got into the car and his driver closed the door, but Spud rolled down the window. "How old are you, Annie?"

"I'm fourteen, almost fifteen, sir, er — Spud."

"And Elisabeth?"

"She's sixteen. She missed a lot of school in Holland

because of the war." Didn't want him to think she was slow. "Elisabeth is my best friend." I had to stifle a giggle because I could see her at the window watching us.

I heard a big sigh from Mr. Spud, and then he broke into a wide grin. "Annie, do me a favor. Y'all tell her to wait for me. Tell her Rory Lee Murphy will be back for her when she's eighteen." And with that he rolled up the window, but I swear I could hear him yell "Yee-haw" all the way to the end of the block.

Chapter 19

The spunk-and-gumption Annie Howard would have skipped back into the house and bombarded Daddy with all the reasons we had to phone Spud Murphy right away and call that magic number to find out about guide dogs. But something told me not to rush. I needed to take time to see things a bit clearer. For just a few moments I'd had a glimpse of the old Daddy, the silly goofball not afraid to tease an old buddy. But that fellow didn't hang around very long. He was replaced by a more timid version, whose voice got a tremor just talking about getting out in the big wide world again.

Instead, I put the card in my butterfly box, the one that held all my treasures. I'd wait a bit and talk to Grandma first and maybe Uncle Billy. Rushing ahead and nagging Daddy about making big decisions probably wasn't the best plan. It occurred to me that after all Daddy had been through, he might feel safer staying put and letting us be his connection with the outside world.

Johannes had also been on my mind. It seemed like ages since I'd seen him. Was he afraid of what lay ahead, too? The little flashes of that other Johannes, the angry one, still scared me. Was his rage the battle he was fighting now? Were there monsters in his head he feared, especially ones that looked too much like him?

Elisabeth and I had never talked about Holland and the war, but that changed the following week after what happened at school.

We were at our usual table in a corner of the cafeteria when the ever-so-charming Marlene Joyner slithered by in her new Lanz dress and red Capezio flats. She wasn't going to miss a chance to make fun of Elisabeth.

"Well," she said in a Betty Boop voice that must have reached at least half the lunch room, "If it isn't Heidi and what's-her-name. Little Miss Kiss-Up, the teacher's pet." Her petticoats bounced, and with her hands on her hips she sa-shayed over to the popular girls' table and sat down to howls of laughter. She whispered something, and the girls all started talking over each other in phony German accents.

Ordinarily, I wouldn't have budged, just ignored Marlene and the others. She wasn't worth bothering with. But something in me exploded. I was going to get even. Snobs like them I could handle. But no one, especially Elisabeth, deserved being humiliated like that. I shot out of my chair so fast it fell over with a loud whack. My face burned and my fists clenched. I turned around and marched toward their table. I swear I saw them flinch. The peals of laughter ended abruptly.

Elisabeth followed on my heels and began tugging my arm. "Let us go, Annie. Please!"

I shook her off and stepped right up to Marlene. "You are about the meanest, stupidest person I've ever met." I put my face right up next to hers, my balled-up fists tight against my thighs. "Lay off! You don't know anything. Elisabeth VanderVelde is one of the bravest people I know. Braver than you'll ever be." I shook my finger right in front of Marlene's snotty little nose. "So leave her alone, or you'll have to answer to me."

Elisabeth was standing next to me, her hands covering her face, trembling. I took her arm and realized I wasn't so steady myself. As we passed by our table, I swept up what was left of our chicken salad sandwiches, and we strode off and out to the softball field. It was that very afternoon Elisabeth finally told me about her own monsters, but first she had a few words for me.

"Annie, I never see you act so," she said, settling herself on the closest stone bench. "It was not to my liking."

Maybe I'd expected her to be thrilled at my bravery or at least thank me, but I had to admit, I didn't feel so good about telling Marlene off. As a matter of fact, I felt a little sick to my stomach. "I'm sorry if I upset you. Marlene just made me so mad." My excuse sounded dumb even to me. I stood there digging my toe into the grass. Then I straightened up. "I know what, let's leave. I'll go to the office and tell the secretary you're sick, and I'm going to ride the bus home with you."

And so we did just that. The ladies in the principal's office were too busy looking after a seventh grade boy who'd just thrown up his lunch in the secretary's wastebasket to pay too much attention to us.

On the bus ride to the VanderVeldes', neither of us said a word. Elisabeth just stared out the window. Tante Dee met us at the door, and although she seemed surprised to see us, she just bustled around making tea and said she would call Grandma and tell her where I was.

Once we got to her bedroom with our tea and a plate of sugar cookies, Elisabeth started to cry. I felt bad and didn't know what to do, so I just sat in what she called her slipper chair and nibbled on a cookie. I had no taste for it, so I put it down and waited.

"You are better person than Marlene and her friends," she said in between sobs. "You must not poison yourself with anger." She quickly wiped away tears with her fingers, and after a few swallows of tea, she began her own story.

The day her parents were killed she had been out looking for food, spending the morning digging in the gardens of abandoned farms for roots or anything edible. She and Johannes had fought, silly stuff. It was their birthday, and he was acting like a spoiled brat.

"I am very mad at him, so I run out to the fields. Later when I hear motorcycles, I don't know what to do." Elisabeth stopped and studied her hands. "I know what such a sound means. I decide perhaps if I just make it to our barn, Jon will find me and know what is best to do." She swallowed hard and hesitated before going on. "I saw the German soldier before he saw me, and I knew he would not hesitate to shoot me. As I got nearer, I hear shots. I cover my ears. Just concentrate on getting to Jon, I tell myself. I see soldiers' bodies. The first thing I know is they are just boys, with faces dark and bloody. So much dying!" Elisabeth sucked in another breath, and made a swipe at the tears trickling off her chin.

I went to sit next to her on the bed and stroked her hair. Her braids had come undone and hung in wavy strands around her face. "You don't need to tell me any more."

"No, Annie, I need to make you understand." She tugged at her braids and handed me her comb. "Jon would not let me near our house. I do not see my parents again until we bury them. I am very sad. Jon, he is like a boy made of ice. We go to hide under a broken bridge for days. I am so afraid, I cry but cannot speak. Jon does not shed a tear. He is cold and silent until one of our tantes finds us and tells us all the soldiers are leaving because it is said the Allied troops are coming." She took in a deep breath and went quiet, except for the occasional sob. "He softens a little, but the hardness stays, until he meets you."

I knew then that she had heard Johannes that night in the greenhouse. Carefully, I continued to work on her braids, combing out each snarl and tangle. We sat like that until the room began to darken. By the time Tante Dee tapped on the door, Elisabeth had stopped crying and her face had turned rosy again.

"Your uncle is here for you, Annie," said Tante Dee through the door. "I tell him you be out in some minutes. I have poured him coffee."

I opened the door. A quick glance seemed to assure Tante Dee that Elisabeth was all right. We both got one of Tante's sweet smiles. Before scurrying back to the kitchen, she wrapped me in a quick hug and was gone before I could thank her.

"Will you be all right, Elisabeth?" I asked. "I hate to go home and leave you here full of all these terrible memories of the war."

She reached for her violin. "I have Bach and Mr. Mozart," she said, rubbing at a spot on the wood. "They never get angry or puff up like old hens." And already there was just a hint of a twinkle in her eyes. "I play you something so you go home with a quiet heart." And she tucked the violin under her chin, tightened the strings, and soon the room was filled with music.

Chapter 20

Seemed like a million things were bouncing around in my brain. I had to sit down and try to sort them all out before I even thought of talking to anyone else. Made me wish I were eleven again when I could figure things out with my old imaginary friend Mr. Truman. What a silly goose I'd been! I mean, thinking I could make the president appear whenever I needed him. Well, I wasn't a kid anymore. Fourteen-year-olds did not conjure up the president for heart-to-heart talks. Besides, I bet President Truman had lots to do these days, what with worrying about all those Communists running everyone ragged.

Now that I could add Elisabeth along with Daddy and Johannes to my worry list, I had plenty on my mind. It was enough to make a person want to run and jump in bed and burrow down into the covers. But I intended to keep up my end of the deal with Mr. Spud. So a few days after Elizabeth told me her story, I went looking for Grandma. I found her all wrapped up in an old quilt, sound asleep in the wicker rocker, a book open on the little table next to her. That talk with Mr. Spud was stuck in my head, and just when I opened my mouth to tell her my plans for Daddy, the phone rang. I ran out to the hall to answer it.

It was Dee VanderVelde for Grandma. Something had gotten her so excited that I could barely understand a word. My heart did a flip when she mentioned Johannes. Was he hurt, sick? What? She finally made it clear. We were all to join them for the Daffodil Parade. Many of the flowers decorating the floats would be from a family farm.

"Well, I'll be," said Grandma Hattie when she put down the phone. "Did you know those folks ended up in Tacoma to be near Hendrik's older brother Theo and his wife? They came here before the war and started a bulb farm in Puyallup." She'd barely hung up when the phone rang again. "My land, now who's that?"

It was Elisabeth. "Annie, do say you'll come with us to the parade. We will sit in a special place with Uncle Theo." I could hear voices in the background. "We will see the floats with Uncle's flowers."

"Will Johannes be there too?" A long silence. I waited for Elisabeth's answer, hoping it would be the one I wanted.

"Tante says she can't promise he will be, but she will try. Do say you'll come."

It was good to hear Elisabeth go on so cheerfully about daffodils, but I was half-listening, wondering if I would ever see Johannes again. Had telling me about his parents and the soldiers wounded his spirit? Was he even now staying away because he couldn't face his anger? Or worse, was he afraid to face me? What if nothing I did or said was enough? I couldn't let him just slip out of my life.

When Mama got home, Grandma told her all about our invitation to the Daffodil Parade and how we would be seated in a special place. Didn't take much effort to persuade Mama. She was certain that "special" meant all kinds of important people. It was the kind of occasion that turned her into a charming social butterfly — my favorite side of Mama.

After dinner, her arms up to her elbows in soapsuds, she suddenly turned to me and Grandma and suggested having the VanderVeldes over for dinner after the parade. Since Grandma Hattie's wrist was still in a cast and Mama wasn't the best cook in the world, I wondered just how we were going to manage a dinner party.

"You've both talked so much about the family, it's time I meet them, and this would be a way to thank them." Mama turned to me with a big old smile on her face.

"Why Dory, that's a fine idea. I'll drag myself out to the phone in a bit and give Dee a call." Grandma gave me her "look," the one with the raised eyebrows that signaled, "What's your mama up to?" Mama either hadn't noticed or had ignored Grandma's lack of enthusiasm. We both knew who would be expected to do most of the cooking.

"What's a fine idea, Ma?" Billy was standing in the doorway, a dead cigar clamped in his teeth. He knew better than to actually smoke it in front of Grandma.

"Take that disgusting thing out of your mouth, Billy Howard, and maybe we'll extend you an invitation." Grandma reached over with her left hand and moved her right a bit. I winced right along with her. "Dr. Miller does a fine job with broken wrists, but I've no doubt that's one of his cigars you're chomping on."

The cigar quickly disappeared, and I wondered if Billy had stowed it away in his pocket. "OK, Ma, now what are you three gals planning?"

Before Grandma could answer, I piped up. "We're having the VanderVeldes over for dinner after the Daffodil Parade, and we took a vote. You're cooking."

"I see," said Billy, a faint smile twitching at his lips. "Sure, why not? I can make my hobo stew, easiest thing in the world." He took a little bow. "Am I allowed to ask a guest? If so, my vote is for a certain school teacher."

"For Pete's sake, Billy. Honestly!" And I stomped off to do my algebra homework.

Mama had me up and out in the kitchen first thing the next

morning. I had the bacon frying before Grandma was even up. Uncle Billy took over the rest of breakfast, and we all sat down to a Sunday morning feast. Mama was being her usual bossy self, acting like she was the only one in the world who knew a thing about a kitchen.

Even so, Grandma was awfully cheerful, despite her sore wrist. "I'll phone Dee and Hendrik after I finish my breakfast. I need to call Gloria as well and tell her she and Will have to take care of the store a bit longer."

Uncle Billy made it clear he most certainly intended to invite Miss Moore. Maybe I could find a way to keep that from happening. Of course, he didn't even know her number.

"You can invite her for me, first thing tomorrow. OK, kid?" Uncle Billy started clearing breakfast dishes and whistling "The More I See You."

What was it with this family? All we needed now was for the ever-so-charming Gardenia Man to show up at the dinner party. Criminy!

On Saturday when the VanderVeldes arrived to take us all to the parade, Daddy insisted on staying home. I needn't have worried about seeing Johannes; he wasn't with them. "He caught a cold in Canada," explained Auntie Dee, when I squeezed in the back seat of the Lincoln to sit beside Elisabeth, right across from Mama and Grandma. "He had a fever, so I tell him he must stay at home." I couldn't help but wonder if that was really and truly the reason.

Turned out it was Mama who had the most fun that day. Although she never saw the mayor or his wife or any other "really important" people, she clapped and oohed and ahhed more than any of us. She even seemed genuinely interested when Elisabeth's Uncle Theo explained about bulb growing and the history of the parade.

Uncle Billy and Miss Moore arrived late and left early. "Have to go home and get that stew on," he told Grandma as he pushed his way past us.

I wondered if he was going to ask Miss Moore to peel the potatoes. Thank goodness "Larry" didn't show up that afternoon, but his flowers did. We arrived home to a big bouquet of roses. At least they weren't gardenias. Uncle Billy was true to his word, and he had a big pot of stew cooking and a pan of cornbread baking in the oven. Miss Moore was nowhere to be seen. She'd gone home to change.

The VanderVeldes were all smiles and laughter as they dropped us off after the parade, and when they came back later for dinner, they had a basketful of cookies and little frosted cakes, just the thing to make Grandma forget about her wrist for a while. "Oh, Dee, all my favorite pastries," she whooped. I thought for a minute Grandma might dance a jig.

When the doorbell rang a second time, Uncle Billy went for the front door like a streak. I didn't bother to tell him that he had flour all over his tie. And that was another thing. I'd almost never seen him wear a tie before, let alone cook wearing one.

Mama was the perfect hostess, even to the point of wearing the blue dress she'd left in the back of the closet since Daddy came back from the war — his favorite. Something was going on with her, but I hadn't figured it out yet.

She'd even made one of her layered Jell-O salads in individual molds, sparkling like jewels at every place. Not a lopsided one in the bunch. Something was definitely going on.

The biggest surprise came after dinner. Well, watching Uncle Billy drool over Miss Moore to the point of accidentally pouring ice water down her front was the high point of the evening. Elisabeth and I giggled endlessly and pinched each other under the table.

Miss Moore, it turned out, played the piano. I was surrounded by musicians. Afraid she might ask me to sing, I jumped at the chance to clear the dessert plates. I couldn't carry a tune in a bucket.

"I bet you have a lovely singing voice, Lydia," said Grandma. "Do you know 'It Might as Well Be Spring'?"

And Miss Lydia Moore sang it through, with Daddy adding his sweet voice at the end. I swear Uncle Billy was hovering about three feet off the floor. Geez Louise! If this got out at school, that my uncle was seeing the art teacher, I'd never hear the end of it.

Uncle Hendrik stood up, nodding to us all, "If you permit me, please. Miss, do you know the melody to 'We'll Meet Again'?"

"Of course! It was my father's favorite." Miss Moore ran her fingers down the keys and began to play, but it was Uncle Hendrik's voice that caught everyone's attention. I watched Grandma's face. That song had brought her to tears many times while Daddy was missing in action.

When he had finished, the room went quiet. Grandma broke the silence with "Bravo! Bravo!" Uncle Hendrik took a bow. "Good Heavens! What a voice. You sound like Nelson Eddy." Grandma was in seventh heaven. "How do you know that song?"

By now Uncle Hendrik's face was as red as his socks. "I hear it many times after the Allies come. It stays with me because we are delivered from the Nazis and we can finally breathe our own breath again. Those boys leave. I know I never see again."

Elisabeth started to correct his English, but I grabbed her hand. We all knew what he meant.

I looked around the room. Tante Dee and Hendrik VanderVelde held hands, their eyes sparkling. Daddy had his arm around Mama, and Billy was leaning over the piano, mooning over Miss Moore. Grandma reached over and patted my hand. "A perfect evening. I should break my wrist more often."

Miss Moore closed the piano lid and stood up, a mile-wide smile on her face. "A perfect evening to be sure, but I have the best news of all. Annie, Elisabeth, both of you have made the All-City Young Artists Exhibit! One of Annie's watercolors and a pen and ink drawing of Elisabeth's." The whole room broke out in applause.

Mama fluttered around the room a bit, picking up glasses and cups. Suddenly, she turned. "This *has* been such a lovely evening. Dee, Hendrik, Lydia, Elisabeth — it has been such a pleasure to invite you into our home. I'd like to take advantage of this festive mood and make an announcement of my own."

I could only roll my eyes. Mama wasn't about to let Miss Moore hog the limelight. Maybe the fire chief's wife had come into the shop. But what came next made me light-headed.

Mama took Daddy's hand. "Eddie and I would like to share our news. In the fall we will be welcoming a new baby." Daddy pulled Mama tighter and gave her a kiss right in front of everybody.

With that absolutely disgusting news, I did the only thing I could. I walked right out of the room, and on my way, accidentally on purpose, I took a swipe at the vase of roses on the buffet, knocking them to the floor with an ear-splitting crash.

Chapter 21

"Ma figured you might be out here." Uncle Billy stood in the doorway of the workshop, still in his good clothes, shifting his feet and rubbing at spots of stew on his new shirt. "You ought to know your grandma's in there covering for you. What's got into you, kid?"

I was huddled deep into the old armchair breathing in wood smells and wax, not wanting to talk to a soul, but of course, Uncle Billy wasn't going leave me alone.

He took out a handkerchief and brushed the pine curls off the workbench and sat down. He was clearly settling in for a full explanation.

"She told the VanderVeldes you had an upset stomach. They were too busy fussing over your mama to notice your grand exit." He rubbed at his jaw for a bit. "I agree, the news is unexpected and maybe a little hard to take in at first, but . . ."

"It's disgusting," I said, cutting him off and burrowing

deeper into the chair.

"C'mon, Annie, Be happy for your folks. Your dad's real excited; he's already making plans for a crib."

"They're way too old," I said, not brave enough to tell Uncle Billy what I was really thinking.

"Yeah, they probably seem that way to you, but believe me, kiddo, they're definitely not over the hill." His face turned into a big smile and he started to laugh little bark-like yips until I shocked him into silence.

"In the war, Billy — did you ever kill a person? I mean did you ever see the soldier's face and shoot him dead?"

Uncle Billy pulled his face tight. "Dang, Annie! Where'd that come from?"

I took in a deep breath and told him everything Johannes had told me. When I'd finished, I was shaking all over and afraid I just might puke hobo stew all over that spanking new tie.

"That's tough, Annie Leigh." Uncle Billy did a whole lot of throat clearing and concentrated on toeing some sawdust for a bit. "Poor kid, Jon couldn't have been more than ten, eleven, and he's been carrying that around with him all these years."

I studied a pile of oak planks and mulled over the next question. "I mean, how do you just kill a person?"

Uncle Billy didn't hesitate. "You don't think you have a choice, and you sure don't have time to weigh the right or wrong of it. Jon didn't have much of a choice, did he? Those Nazis had already shot his folks and were about to shoot Elisabeth and most likely him as well."

With that my uncle pulled out a pack of Juicy Fruit gum and handed me a stick. "You're not going to let this rest. I know you, so here goes." Uncle Billy put two sticks in his mouth at once. He chewed a while and then began. "The first time I saw the man I killed, I did look him straight in the eyes, close enough to see one of those red strawberry birthmarks just under his left eye. I've never forgotten that. I shot him and then tossed my guts all over my boots. I wasn't much older than Jon is right now. The next time a pang, but after that — nothing. "

"Don't tell me any more, Billy." His lower lip had been trembling, and his voice was all shaky and high. "That's OK."

"No, it isn't kid. Your mother will probably have my hide, but maybe it's time you understood more about what your dad, and your old uncle, and even Jon and Elisabeth have witnessed. So here goes. Your dad and I were part of a highly trained army. A good soldier never asks why. Discipline is what keeps you going. You're trained not to think, only to react. In battle you don't have time to think."

Uncle Billy stood up and grabbed a Coke out of the old fridge he kept in the workshop. "I can't imagine what it was like for the VanderVeldes. Living all those years under the Nazis, starving to death, never able to feel safe. They were barely surviving. That's what Jon did when he pulled that trigger. He was fighting for survival, his and Elisabeth's." Uncle Billy took a big swallow of cola and held out the bottle. I shook my head. "What's more, Jon wasn't part of a disciplined army; he had to develop some survival skills all on his own. The Nazi occupation was his boot camp. I can't guarantee you that what Jon has been through, what he did, won't sit in his gut, in his heart for the rest of his life. But look, he made an important decision when he told you what happened. That was pretty brave, don't you think?"

"I guess so."

After pulling at his hair this whole time, Uncle Billy looked a little wild. He hadn't talked to me like that since he made amends to Gloria and Grandma for his rotten behavior the year I lived in Walla Walla.

"For now, let's keep this little talk to ourselves," said Billy. "Let's go in and see if you can muster up some enthusiasm and show your mama you're happy for her." He put his arm around me and gave my shoulder a squeeze. "If you're real good, I'll even make you one of my toddies."

"Toddies are for bad colds and flu, not for celebration. And what will Grandma think?" I said, my voice barely a whisper. "I'm not sick; I've just got a whole lot of stuff to figure out."

"Never mind, kid. If ever a night called for something stronger than cocoa, this is it."

Chapter 22

A week went by, and I was a total wreck. I'd run Uncle Billy's words around in my head a thousand times. I kept thinking back to that summer in Walla Walla, the morning in Grandma's store when Billy's friend Scooter and I were stacking soup cans. He'd tried to make me understand what had sent Billy home so full of rage. Near the end of the war, Billy had been rescued alive, his buddies dead all around him. How did a person turn off all that sorrow, all that hate, all that death, that horror? If you went empty inside to survive, how did you turn your life back on? Somehow my uncle had found a way.

On the morning of the art contest, Miss Moore signed me out of all my morning classes to help her install our entries at the Central Library. She probably didn't need me — there were only six pictures — but she made it all sound very important.

The wall she'd reserved was in the best light, she'd made sure of that. "It wouldn't do to get stuck in some dark corner," she said, stepping away from my watercolor. "This is lovely. You have a great sense of color, Annie. And watercolor isn't an easy medium."

For some reason, without warning, sobs began to form in my throat. I was about to blubber all over the place. Just like that. A cloud burst.

"Oh my, Annie! I hope those are cries of joy." Miss Moore hesitated a minute. And before I could protest, she put her arm around me and walked me down the hall to the ladies' room.

Once inside, I couldn't hold back. The tears came in buckets. The words I'd needed to let out, a bunch of questions I didn't have the answers to, just came out in a rush of burps and gulps.

Miss Moore didn't say anything the whole time. She just leaned against the sink and listened until my sobs slowed down to a few gasps. She fished a hanky out of her pocket and rinsed it in cold water. "Here, hold this over your eyes for a bit."

The faint scent of lavender made me feel a whole lot better. Miss Moore rinsed out the hanky again and dabbed at my face. "That's a lot to have packed into that young head of yours."

She picked up the jacket she'd hastily thrown over a stall and smiled at me. "Take a few minutes, and when you're ready, meet me out at the car."

As I stumbled down the stairs and out of the library, I was thinking, You acted like a big dumb cluck — and right in front of Miss Moore.

Lydia Moore was standing next to her car smoking a cigarette. "You caught me," she said, her cheeks turning bright pink. "I'm afraid it's a bad habit I picked up during my student days in France."

I must have had a funny look on my face because Miss Moore blushed again. "Oh, I've shocked you," she said, taking out a mint tin from her pocket. "Of course, you probably have heard what caused the dismissal of Miss Parker." She took a long drag on her cigarette and paused to flick off the ash end. She snapped the stub into the tin and put it into her pocket. "Smoking is about as daring as I can manage." She opened the car door. "Come on. I'll treat you to a hamburger and a cherry Coke at that little place next to the Pantages Theater. What's it called . . . Richard's?" She looked at me for a second before starting the car. "I can't give you nice, neat answers to some of those questions, but I can at least hear you out."

It was only eleven, so we had the restaurant nearly to ourselves. We sat at the very end of the counter, away from the other two customers. Miss Moore picked at her hamburger and listened carefully while I told her about what I wanted for Daddy and why it was a troublesome topic at home. I said very little about Johannes and made no mention of the complications with dopey Gardenia Man. In between bites I stumbled through some of my conversation with Elisabeth. Every so often Miss Moore would stop me and ask a question that got me to thinking, but one last question stumped me.

"Annie, that's such a lot for you to solve on your own. Sounds as if your uncle is a good listener, and wise, too. But what do you want?" My uncle's ears must have been burning.

"Well, like I told you, I want to help Daddy be more independent."

Miss Moore reached over and touched my shoulder. "Yes, Annie, I understand that, but what do *you* want for yourself? I want you to think about that."

On the way back to school, I thought about Miss Moore's question. No one had ever asked me what I wanted. Mama sent me to Grandma's the spring my appendix burst. I stayed the good part of a year. She never once asked me if that's what I really and truly wanted. At the time it wasn't what I wanted.

"Now," said Miss Moore, as she pulled her old coupe into the school parking lot and turned off the ignition. "Let me just say this. I can't and shouldn't tell you how to feel or what to believe. I can only share with you what I witnessed my year in France soon after the war." She continued to look straight ahead but paused and took in a deep breath. Her voice was low and even. "Wars change people. Their very souls are tested. The will to survive causes them to act in ways foreign to them in peacetime. Many of the young men and women I met in Paris had been forced to grow up fast. They had stopped feeling and found it painful to acknowledge any kind of emotion again when the war was over. All that loss was too much to bear."

I thought about how close we'd come to losing Daddy, and my stomach knotted up. I didn't know what to say to Miss Moore, so I said nothing. We walked from the teachers' lot past the ball field in silence. Once inside the front hall, I stopped at my locker and fiddled with the combination, thinking about how so many had lost so much.

Miss Moore stopped as well and looked straight at me. Her eyes were huge. "Let the adults in your life work out some of this turmoil. You have a kind and loving nature, but you aren't responsible for everyone else's happiness. It's not necessarily selfish to think about wanting something for yourself." Then she turned and walked down the hall toward her classroom. I stood there, wondering when, if ever, the war would truly leave us.

Uncle Billy and Grandma and I rushed through dinner. Daddy said he would clear up. He wasn't going to the exhibit. He insisted he needed to polish a side table they had refinished. I wondered if the real reason was that he didn't want to be left out while everyone else was going on about what they were looking at.

Mama would join us after work. I noticed Uncle Billy had his hair slicked back again. I wasn't about to tell him he looked a lot like George Raft in one of those gangster movies. Grandma was in a peculiar mood. She would whisper something to Daddy or Billy and then giggle like a kid. Maybe she was feeling giddy after having her cast taken off that morning.

Somehow we made it, and by six thirty we were at the Central Library in our Sunday best. Grandma offered to stay out front to wait for Mama, but Uncle Billy, the goof, took off for the stairs. He couldn't even wait for the elevator.

When I reached the second floor and the elevator doors opened, I could see he'd already cornered Miss Moore. "Annie," she called out, with a little chirp in her voice. "Come see." She was standing in front of my watercolor. A red ribbon was attached to the corner of the frame. I had won second place.

"Geez, Annie, don't look so disappointed!" Uncle Billy scolded. "That's a really neat picture of Ma's store you painted, and you can't knock second place."

Miss Moore grabbed my hands in both of hers. For a minute I thought she was going to swing me around. "I'm immensely pleased, aren't you?" She pulled me down to Elisabeth's drawing of a Dutch village. "Look, a blue ribbon! She's won first prize. You two are the big winners!"

I looked around. Where were Mama and Grandma? They should have been here by now. All kinds of families were standing around in clumps, admiring pictures and gabbing about the prizes. Children were running around, and Uncle Billy had found the punch and cookies.

"Come with me," said Miss Moore, and she carefully guided me across the room to the reception table where she picked up a bouquet of lavender roses and handed them to me. "The nicest man just brought these for you and a dozen pink ones for Elisabeth."

It was then that I saw Johannes, as well as Elisabeth, holding her bouquet, all smiles. Johannes started over toward me. It seemed like forever since I'd seen him, and his eyes seemed to be especially blue when they caught mine. But over Johannes's shoulder I caught a glimpse of Gardenia Man. So that's why Mama was late. She was probably somewhere powdering her nose. I looked over at Uncle Billy, but he was too busy trying to impress Miss Moore to notice anyone else. How dare Mama bring that awful florist to the exhibit!

My face felt hot, and for a minute I couldn't get my breath. I dropped the roses at Miss Moore's feet and ran out and down the stairs. No way was I going to risk running into Mama in the elevator. And Grandma? She'd probably gone back home in disgust.

"Annie, stop! Wait — I come with you." To my surprise it was Johannes, right on my heels.

I stopped outside the library to catch my breath. Johannes

grabbed my arm. "Annie, I must talk to you. Where are you going?"

"Wherever that bus is going." I took his hand, and together we ran down to the corner. The doors unfolded, and we both jumped on and fell into the first seat.

As the bus pulled away, Johannes smiled and pointed out the window. "Look, your mama and your grandmother are helping that lady into a wheelchair."

I leaned over Johannes and looked out. He was right. A taxi pulled away, and there were Mama and Grandma fussing over a pretty blond woman in a red coat in a wheelchair. And coming down the library steps was Gardenia Man with Uncle Billy and Mr. VanderVelde. My world suddenly made absolutely no sense to me at all.

Chapter 23

For a split second I was ready to jump up, yank the cord, and bring the bus to a grinding halt. I had a mind to jump off and run right back up the hill to demand that Mama explain what she and Gardenia Man were up to right there and then. But warning voices filled my head. I mean, did I really want to hear that she and dopey Larry were going to run off together like the choir director at our church in Seattle and Mrs. Hammond, my fifth-grade gym teacher? And what about Daddy? Had he really missed the exhibit because he found out Mama didn't care about him after all and was going to have Larry's love child? Those voices didn't seem to have the faintest idea what Grandma, Uncle Billy, and Mr. VanderVelde, not to mention red coat lady in the wheelchair, had to do with any of it.

Johannes had slipped his arm around me and held me close. He hadn't said a word since we'd turned down Eleventh Street. And what had he been up to the last few weeks? Still, just being near him made me feel jumpy and all tingly, like a million little ant feet running relays on my arms.

After a few harsh words from the bus driver, we made the right transfer, but then practically missed my stop. We got off the bus at Wolfe's Market just as a fire truck passed us and disappeared around the corner.

"Great," I said, "I bet they had to rescue one of Mrs. Hinkle's scraggly tomcats from the storm drain again."

But it wasn't the Hinkles' cat. It was Daddy. Not in the storm drain, but sitting out on the front steps with Dr. Miller, who had his stethoscope up against Daddy's chest. I dropped Johannes's hand and rushed over to the porch. "What's going on? Why was the fire truck here?" Johannes, thinking straighter than I was, immediately took off his jacket and helped Daddy into it.

He was breathing in funny short puffs like he'd just run a mile. Dr. Miller took my arm and pulled me aside. "Where's your mother?" That was a good question. One I wasn't sure how to answer. "She's downtown at the library," I stammered. Even to me, it sounded dumb.

Dr. Miller picked up Daddy's wrist, all the while making funny harrumph sounds. "Your dad won't hear of going over to Tacoma General for some tests just to be safe, but his color's good and he isn't vomiting. Let's hope he didn't inhale enough smoke to cause real trouble."

Just when I thought things couldn't get any crazier, Harry and Ella Mae Hinkle came strolling out our front door. She had a mop in one hand and a bucket in the other. "We were trying to get the kitchen cleaned up a bit before your mama saw the mess. And I mean mess." She took the edge of her apron and wiped a smudge of soot off of Harry's chin for emphasis. "Why, if our Hal hadn't been taking his evening stroll down the back alley this evening, your whole house might a burned right down to the ground."

Mr. Hinkle made little humming sounds and patted Ella Mae on the shoulder. She leaned over to wring out the mop over Mama's prized hydrangeas. "We'll stick around 'til Dorothy gets here, dearie. You stay with your daddy. Harry and I'll go in and open some more windows and air out the place. The whole house smells like a fall bonfire in there."

I looked at Daddy. "The kitchen caught on fire?" My voice sounded high notes exactly like Mama's. I shut my mouth pretty fast.

Poor proud Daddy. He seemed to collapse into a heap at my feet. "I was just trying to get things ready," he wheezed. "I promised your mama I'd have no trouble getting some of my chili started for the party, but I don't know what happened. I stoked the fire some and sparks must have jumped out and caught something." He let out a string of little bark-like coughs. "Dang bust it, that old stove! Thank God for Ella Mae.

I'll never call her a nosey parker again."

"Party? What party, Daddy?"

Before Daddy could answer, Dr. Miller waved me off and motioned to Johannes to help him take Daddy up to the porch swing. We were just getting him settled when cars started pulling up. First Uncle Billy, Grandma, and Elisabeth showed up in the pickup. She had our winning ribbons in her hand. The VanderVeldes arrived in the grand town car, and Mama and disgusting Larry got out first. Uncle Hendrik took the wheelchair out and he and Tante Dee helped the blond lady into her chair. Miss Moore arrived in that ancient black Studebaker of hers.

I wanted to grab Daddy and disappear, but that was impossible. What would I say to Grandma and Miss Moore? I'd been such a pill. Everyone started talking at once. Mama started to cry. I was about to tell Gardenia Man to go fly a kite when he picked up blond lady and Uncle Hendrik grabbed the wheelchair and everyone began to squeeze onto our little front porch.

"Well, this isn't exactly the celebration we'd planned," said Uncle Billy. "When you said you were going to make your super hot chili, Eddie, we didn't expect you needed to set the house on fire to do it." He made little heh! heh! sounds at his own joke and turned to me. "Where'd you two lovebirds fly off to? I was afraid you'd go and miss your own party."

I felt my cheeks flush. "Lovebirds. Jeepers, Billy!"

But no one was paying any attention. Least of all Johannes. He had already started helping Tante Dee take trays of food out of the Lincoln. Mama was fluttering around Daddy, while Grandma urged everyone to move into the house.

Except for the smell, the living and dining rooms were in fine shape. Well, there was that fine layer of soot on the china. Daddy had put out Mama's best lace tablecloth, and the plates and silverware laid out in Daddy's higgledy-piggledy style on the sideboard.

"Oh, my pantry!" screamed Mama, having moved into the kitchen. "My lovely powder blue walls! My new curtains!"

I don't know what exactly Ella Mae had cleaned up, but one half of the kitchen was a scorched mess. The rest, except for all the water and that ton of soot, was fine. As if she had just read my mind, Ella Mae leaned on the mop, took a look around, and announced to everyone scrunched into the kitchen, "You should have seen it before my Harry and I gave it a going over."

Grandma moved close to me, and I leaned in for a kiss. "Later, missy," she whispered, "I want an explanation for your sudden escape from the library, but now I need you to help get this shindig started." She turned to search for an old tea towel to clean off the dining table. "I'm not even sure you deserve this party after that little stunt."

I stood there in the kitchen, the place that had always been my safe haven, and for a minute wished everyone but Daddy would just disappear. Mama was moving around trying to shoo folks back into the living and dining rooms. I went to grab a clean rag out of the linen closet so I could start wiping off all the plates and silverware. Grandma rolled up the tablecloth and wiped down the table in a jiffy, and Tante Dee began to arrange all the platters and trays of food.

I found myself shoved up against blond lady in the wheelchair. She took my hand in her soft, silky one. "Annie, dear Annie. In all this confusion we haven't met, and I've been so looking forward to meeting you." Her voice was soft and silky as her hand. "I'm Isabella Capaldi, Larry's wife. Everyone calls me Belle."

I just stood there like a dummy, my mouth opening and closing like a dying fish. Holy cow! Gardenia Man's wife. Holy cow!

And before I could get my wits together, Grandma suddenly waltzed over with a big Cheshire grin on her face and yelled, "Surprise!"

And there she was. Just when I needed her most. Miss Gloria. She pulled me into the warmest, best lavender-smelling hug I'd had in a very long time. My head stopped spinning and the knots in my stomach came untied, and I swear, my world slipped right back into place with one sharp, solid click.

Chapter 24

Grandma never found out my real reason for running off the night of the art awards. How could I tell her that all along I was certain Mama and Mr. Capaldi — certainly couldn't call him Gardenia Man anymore — were having an affair? How embarrassing! And Belle, Mrs. Capaldi, the sweetest thing in the whole world. Never in a million years would I want her to know what a dope I'd been! Turns out Mr. Capaldi had often driven Mama to their house to do Belle's hair or her nails or give her a permanent wave.

What a night of surprises. I hadn't the faintest idea Gloria and Will were coming. No wonder Grandma had been short with me. After we all stood around for a while staring at the scorched walls and each other, Will and Uncle Billy insisted that Daddy go to the hospital for a checkup just to be safe. They helped him out to the limousine, at Uncle Hendrik's insistence, and raced off. I wondered if anyone but me noticed that at the last minute Uncle Billy hopped into Miss Moore's car and they drove off together.

Grandma, Mama, Tante Dee, and Gloria put on aprons and turned into a work crew, mopping up the rest of the water. Larry Capaldi stepped right up and enlisted Johannes to help carry the worst of the kitchen mess out to the backyard. Elisabeth took charge of Lily and pushed her several dizzying turns around the house in her stroller, singing in rapid Dutch. Lily's squeals of laughter filled the rooms.

"I have a confession to make," Mrs. Capaldi confided, taking the rag out of my hand to wipe the last of the soot off the silver. "That school affair when your mother showed up tipsy . . ." she paused and let out the tiniest kid-like giggle. "That was my fault. It was my fortieth birthday, and Larry and I insisted she come to dinner, and well — we did a bit too much celebrating." And then and there she broke into a fit of giggles, and I couldn't do anything but chime in right along with her.

By the time everyone got back from the hospital, the house smelled less of ashes and smoke and more like Pine Sol. And the dining table, mostly thanks to Tante Dee, was set up for a pretty grand feast, considering the fire and all. Good thing, because after Daddy's great adventure and all the excitement, everyone was starving. Ella Mae and Harry even joined us and no one said a word when Ella Mae filled a plate for her Hal.

Later, Uncle Hendrik sat down at the piano, and Elisabeth and Johannes sang to entertain the "menfolk," as Grandma put it. She and Mama put away their mops and went to sort out where our guests were going to stay. I saw Belle pull Lily onto her lap, where she promptly fell asleep. Gloria offered to help me wash the dishes in the bathroom sink, and we kept interrupting each other trying to make up for all the time we'd been apart.

"I want to know all about that boy," insisted Gloria. "He's something special, I can tell."

"We'd be here all night if I started on that. I want to hear everything about Lily."

There would be time to tell Gloria about Johannes, but at that moment I needed to soak up some of that warmth, that pure joy, that loving heart that had always radiated out of her like giant sunrays. For a few minutes I was back in Gloria's room at Grandma's all those years ago, and we were talking and giggling and feeling just plain happy to be in each other's company.

Gloria and I'd barely enough time to catch up when Will came in to see how we were doing. He was holding Lily, who was fast asleep clutching a fuzzy lamb in the fingers that weren't in her mouth. "Annie, hey! Glory, you two almost finished? Everyone's waitin' for you in the parlor." Gloria reached out and took Lily.

"We can put her to bed in my room," I said, and I gave Will the dishtowel and showed him the stack of dishes waiting to be washed. "You won't mind finishing up, Will?"

"Still sassy, I see, Miss Annie," Will said with a wink. "You Howard ladies sure speak your mind."

While Gloria made a nest for Lily among my blankets and pillows so she wouldn't take a tumble off the bed, I was winding up to tell her everything about my plans for Daddy, Elisabeth, Johannes, and whatever else came tumbling out of my frazzled brain.

"I have a feeling we've got lots to talk about," said Gloria. "Let's go say our goodbyes first and then find a real quiet place to have us a sit down."

Out in the living room Uncle Billy was sorting out coats, while Miss Moore sat at the piano, picking out a tune, certainly in no hurry to leave. Tante Dee was at the dining room table, struggling to pack up her dishes. I picked up a stack of bowls and followed Elisabeth out to the car, her arms full of empty platters. Johannes took up the rear carrying a lone cake dish.

"Don't strain a muscle," I said when Johannes caught up with me. "Crystal has lead in it. All that weight, you might hurt yourself."

He looked at me, his raised eyebrows signaling confusion. "Tante's dish is not so heavy . . ." Johannes paused, his eyes sparkling in the bright light of the street lamp. "You make fun.

175

Of course."

Elisabeth had reached the car and was already wrapping dishes in towels and placing them carefully in the trunk. She took my bowls and then the cake dish, muttering something to Johannes in Dutch.

He looked at me, those eyes twinkling even brighter. "She ask me did I need a wheelbarrow. Two against one, I think is not fair."

"Poor Johannes." I grabbed his hand, and he moved closer so he could brush my cheek with a kiss.

Elisabeth started to giggle, and then I did as well. By the time Tante Dee and Uncle Hendrik came down the walk, we were leaning against the car holding our sides from so much laughter. We took a quick poke at one another and then pulled ourselves together.

"Annie, you are always welcome to our house," Uncle Hendrik said with that little bow of his. Tante Dee put a basket into the back seat, hugged me, and steadied herself using my shoulder while I helped her into the front.

Elisabeth climbed into the back, and Johannes grabbed my hand one last time and then followed her. I waved them off and turned to go back into the house, but not before I caught Uncle Billy kissing Miss Moore just as she was about to get into her car. I pretended not to notice.

Back in the house, I found Daddy alone in the living room

listening to his prize, a new Philco radio, standing in a corner of the living room as shiny and grand as a new car.

"Where is everybody?" he asked, turning down the radio. "It's suddenly awfully lonely in here."

"You'll be interested to know that Billy's out front throwing himself at Miss Moore. The VanderVeldes have just left. I think Mama's gone to bed, and I imagine Will and Gloria have gone to settle Lily in Billy's apartment."

Daddy let out a low chuckle. "Billy never learns. Wait 'til he finds out he has to sleep on the couch. Won't be the first time. I imagine he won't even notice if Lydia's on his mind."

"You need anything, Daddy, before you go to bed? Gloria and I are going to spend some time catching up."

"Can't very well ask you to fix me a snack in that kitchen. Dad blast that stove." Daddy reached out, fumbled for a dial, and turned the sound back up on his program. "First thing in the morning Billy and I'll work out the repairs and get started. Task number one: Get a new stove." Daddy turned his cheek up for a goodnight kiss. "I'm going to sit here a while and listen to my sports program, honey. You go enjoy visiting with Gloria."

I was standing in the kitchen when Gloria came back in from Billy's apartment.

"There you are, child," she said, looking past me at the blistered cabinets and stained walls. "Well, at least that awful smell of wet ashes has faded some." Hands on hips, she moved carefully around the room, making clicking noises of distress at every turn. "Land sakes, your mama's fridge looks a right mess. And I'm afraid those fine curtains are past saving." She put her arm around me. "But everyone's safe. That's the main thing. Let's go have us that talk. I told Will I might be a spell."

When we'd settled ourselves in my room, both of us leaning against a stack of pillows on my bed, I figured I'd just have to tell Gloria everything that had been eating at me for weeks. And so I began — starting with Daddy and how I just knew he was hurting, all about Johannes and Elisabeth and how all my joy at knowing them was mixed up with confusion about how to be the very best friend I could be, not to mention how I'd disappointed Elisabeth when I was ready to punch Marlene Joyner, and I still had to work out how I felt about Johannes having actually killed people, even if they were the enemy.

"I mean, Uncle Billy helped me understand some. I know Johannes did the only thing he could to save himself and Elisabeth, but it's still all a bit scary."

Every so often Gloria patted my arm and whispered, "I see."

But mostly she just listened. And finally, I just let it all out and told her what I'd thought about Mama and Mr. Capaldi. I even confessed I'd called him Gardenia Man. By this time I was in tears, but when I looked over at her, Gloria had started to laugh.

"What's so funny? "I croaked.

"Oh, child, I'm not laughing at you. I expect I'm laughing from relief. Come here." And I moved over next to her on the bed, and she pulled me close. "Sweet thing, that's a whole lot to be carrying around all this while."

I leaned my head against Gloria's shoulder and sucked in a big breath, "You mean I'm not a terrible person?"

"My heavens, Annie Leigh, we all make mistakes. What you imagined about your mama was just a silly one and didn't hurt anyone, but maybe yourself. But first let's talk about your friends."

"What do you want to know?"

"Let's start by you remembering how you felt when your daddy was missing."

I looked at Gloria, wondering why she was asking me about that. "Well — I remember I was real sad and really angry, too, and missed him like crazy and tried to wish him home. Sometimes I felt all hollow inside, just a shell walking around."

"And don't forget all those fine conversations with your Mr. Truman. What you and your grandma and your mama were dealing with, child, was loss. But you were lucky to be surrounded by folks who loved you. No enemies threatened you every time you stepped outdoors. You had plenty to eat. A whole family to protect you. And — your daddy came back."

"I don't know if I could have been brave like Johannes and Elisabeth. It's hard to imagine being so young and losing so much."

"It bears thinking about, Annie Leigh. They didn't just lose their family, but everything they held dear. While you were playing war safe in your own backyard or out by your grandma's creek, they were living it. They lost their childhood, their innocence, and their way of life. Everything changed forever." I took a big breath in and tried to grasp all of what Gloria had said. But there was more.

"Children need to feel safe. Imagine never feeling safe and knowing your mama and your daddy can't protect you." Gloria paused. The laughter was gone from her eyes. I figured she wasn't just talking about Johannes and Elisabeth now. "It's difficult enough growing up. In fact, it's mighty hard being a grown-up sometimes. Be patient with your friends. Listen to them. Show them all that joy of yours." Her eyes lit up again. "I don't imagine it will be too difficult to do that, especially with that young man."

Before Gloria could say anymore, I reached over and took her hand and held it tight. I'd always learned a lot from my Miss Gloria, about myself, about acceptance, about love. But I was pretty sure I had tons more to learn.

Chapter 25

Saturday morning we all squeezed into Billy's apartment for breakfast. I'm pretty certain it was the first time my uncle actually had done any cooking in his teeny kitchen on his three-burner electric stove. An old icebox that sat at the top of the stairs didn't even have ice in it. But we made do.

Uncle Billy made his special hash browns and stuck them in the little oven to stay warm. Grandma took her turn and managed bacon and eggs. Gloria made her prize cornbread right on the top of the stove in a skillet. Mama dug around in what was left of our pantry for quite a while looking for her good silver coffee pot, dashing up the garage stairs when she finally found it.

"Not a scratch," she beamed. "Imagine that."

I took Lily out back where a whole patch of huge butter yellow daffodils had come into bloom practically overnight, and we picked a bunch for the picnic table that Billy and Will had set up in the garage. And we all gathered around for a real fine Saturday breakfast.

In between bites, Daddy and Billy talked about their list of things to do and how they planned to start work on the kitchen that very day.

"Next Sunday's Easter," said Daddy. "I'd like to see us at least able to cook a meal in that room by then."

That got Mama and Grandma talking about picking out a new stove that very day.

"Come down to the shop and we can go on my lunch hour, Hattie," said Mama, her eyes shining with excitement and then alarm. "My land, I've got to get to work!" She fluttered around a bit. "How can I leave you all with this mess?"

"We'll be fine, Dory," said Daddy. "Don't take the bus this morning, call a taxi."

"Now that's rich, Eddie, considering the expense this fire's going to cost us."

Leave it to Mama to spoil the moment.

"Don't worry, Dorothy," said Will. "Glory and I can drop you off on our way out of town. We're fixin' to go as soon as we put our valises in the car. Got to get back to Walla Walla and make sure the store is still there. Make sure Scooter's good sense hasn't left him altogether."

"What's the matter with Scooter?" said Daddy, giving Mama a playful swat when she bent down for a kiss on her way back to the house. "He knows that grocery store like the back of his hand."

"Haven't you heard?" said Gloria. "Scooter's in love."

"Who's in love?" Billy asked, having just come down from his apartment with a second pot of coffee. "Are we talking about one Scooter Teeples?"

"Oh, indeed we are," said Gloria. "He's so sweet on Ophelia Bailey, he loses his wits every time she comes into the store."

"Bailey?" I asked. "Is she related to Opal?

"Near as we can tell, Ophelia's her niece. A more genteel side of the family, no doubt," said Will.

Well then we just all burst out with our own stories about Opal and her chewing tobacco and her way with cuss words. I was hoping no one would bring up Gloria's first picnic at Grandma's when Billy showed up drunk and that dreadful Ben Jackson threw rocks and it was all pretty ugly and tense until Opal spit a wad of tobacco almost the length of the backyard. She had not looked kindly on Billy spoiling Grandma's big day. Most folks who knew Gloria and Will would never stand for that kind of ugliness now. Why, just two years back even President Truman had something to say about how colored folks were treated and declared the military had to treat all the soldiers the same. Thankfully, no one brought up that particular July Fourth picnic.

Mama turned up ready for work in the nick of time, and

that was the end of the Opal stories. I walked Lily out to the car, and when Gloria hugged me goodbye, she gave me an extra big squeeze. "You be sure to visit next summer, child. Come as soon as school's out. You can teach Lily how to make hollyhock dolls."

After a round of hugs, Grandma and I walked back to the house and the stack of breakfast dishes that waited for us.

"We have two choices, Sweetpea," said Grandma, letting out a sigh that meant neither was satisfactory. "We can lug all these dishes up those stairs and wash them in that postage stamp-size sink or cart them into the bathroom again."

"What about we wash the dishes right here in the dishpan and rinse them off with water from the hose?"

"Your mama would have a fit." Grandma let out a giggle. "We'll just bring out a bucket of hot water for washing." Grandma looked real pleased with herself. "Bring that garden hose around for the rinse. I'm sure we'll survive, and the day is just warm enough to keep us from pneumonia."

For a good while Grandma and I washed cups and scrubbed egg off plates, hardly saying a word, but I was still thinking about Gloria and what we'd talked about the day before.

"Grandma, do you ever think about how folks treated Gloria when she first came to Walla Walla?"

"It's always there in the back of my mind," said Grandma. "Most particularly when a new customer in the store is rude to her or Will."

"She had a really difficult life before she came to live with us, didn't she?"

"She hasn't shared too much, but I know she was glad to get away from the South and all its ugliness where Negroes were concerned. And of course, she'd lost a lot. First her parents died and then the boy she was going to marry was killed in the war." Grandma let out another one of her big sighs. "Folks at home think a lot of those two, and our friends at church are mighty glad to have them join us every Sunday."

I had so many questions to ask Grandma and ever so many things to talk over with her, but wouldn't you know it, that's when Ella Mae turned up.

"Your phone's been ringing off the hook, missy," she said. "I'm surprised no one's bothered to answer it. Must be pretty important."

I suppose Ella Mae was waiting for an explanation, and we didn't have one. Where were Daddy and Uncle Billy? I wondered. Too bad the workshop phone hadn't been hooked up yet.

I checked out front and realized the pickup was gone. Once in the house, I found a note on the dining room table. Seems those two had already gone off to the hardware store. Just as I was on my way out the back to help Grandma finish up, the phone rang again. I picked it up on the third ring.

"Hello," I said. Silence. Something did a little bounce in my stomach.

"Is this the Howard residence?" The voice sounded so much like my school principal, it gave me a start.

"I'm calling to speak to Edward Howard," said the voice again, solemn as a preacher.

"He isn't at home at the moment. I'm his daughter, Annie. Can I take a message?"

Silence again.

"Is there another adult in the house, Miss?"

"I'm fifteen, sir," I said, fibbing a bit. "Are you the police?" Another plunk in my stomach. I was certain Daddy and Billy had been in an accident.

"No, miss, I'm with the Blinded Veterans Association."

Of course, Mr. Spud wasn't going to let me down. Good for him! Daddy was going to get his dog.

"Is an adult available I can talk to?" Mr. Serious Business said again.

Honestly, I could take a message, especially if it was about Daddy and his chances of getting a guide dog. But Grandma took that moment to walk out into the hall with Daddy's note in her hand.

"Maybe you should take this," I said and handed her the phone. It took me a second to find a paper and pencil, but I was soon ready to take down any details Daddy would need.

Grandma looked puzzled but took the phone. She listened for only a few seconds when all of a sudden her color changed and her eyes grew wide. "I see," she said at one point. Her face grew pale and my heart did a little flip. What could be wrong? Surely Daddy wasn't going to be turned down.

"His family must be devastated," said Grandma, her voice breathy. "No one? No one at all?" Grandma fished a hanky out of her apron pocket. "It was kind of you to let us know." Her face grew pale and my heart did a little flip. "Yes, a number would be good. Eddie will most certainly want to attend the funeral." I handed her the paper and pencil, and she wrote something on the phone pad. "Thank you so much."

Grandma stood looking at the wall for a good long while. When she turned around, I had a feeling I knew what she was going to tell me.

"What happened, Grandma? It's Spud, Mr. Murphy, isn't it?"

I followed Grandma into the living room where she sat down on the sofa and leaned back against the pillows. "Oh, Lordy! Yes, the call was about Mr. Murphy," she said. "Your Mr. Spud must have been really keen on getting your daddy involved in the organization. He'd talked to his buddies about Eddie. That's how they had his number." Grandma let out a big sigh. "How in the world are we going to tell your daddy?"

"Tell him what, Grandma? What's going on?"

"It's so hard to believe, but he was killed last night in a car accident. Both him and his driver. Somehow his dog survived." Grandma dabbed at her eyes. "I barely knew him. We just met, but to think he was right here in this room. Oh my. And to think he has no family. Not a soul."

I went to sit next to Grandma, and we just stayed there frozen, our hands tightly clasped, both picturing the charming, handsome Rory Lee Murphy, his big smile and his big dog Montgomery right there in our living room — and that's where Daddy found us an hour later, our eyes full of tears and our hearts heavy. And how could we tell him, and how could I tell Elisabeth?

Chapter 26

The day before Easter Uncle Billy got up early to wash and wax his pickup to a glittering shine before he drove Daddy out to the VA hospital for Rory Lee Murphy's funeral. Even though Elisabeth had only just met her Mr. Spud, she took his death really hard. So Tante Dee suggested we have our own private service in the garden at their cottage. In the end Elisabeth was the one who decided it would be a special ceremony to mark not only Mr. Murphy's death but that of her mother and father and cousin Herman as well.

Elisabeth knew exactly what she wanted to do. We would plant trees in their memory. I thought it was the very best idea ever. So the morning of the funeral I pulled on pair of old overalls and helped Elisabeth and Johannes dig holes. Uncle Hendrik shouted out instructions like a coach, and we pushed big handfuls of dirt around a dogwood tree for Mama and Papa VanderVelde and a star magnolia for Herman. Mr. Murphy was remembered with a weeping cherry. Elisabeth helped her uncle plant it right near the kitchen garden where she could watch it grow from her window. Uncle Hendrik declared the garden would be a splendid show of color when they all bloomed.

We all had big muddy smudges on our faces and tons of dirt under our nails, not to mention wet, muddy knees, but we still held hands and sang a short hymn in Dutch — well, I hummed along — and Tante Dee said a little prayer before we shed our garden clothes and went into the house for some of her cakes.

Worry still tugged at me. Grandma often used the word fragile to describe someone she was worried about. Was that the right word to describe Elisabeth, maybe even Johannes? And what about Daddy? If so, I had a lot of thinking to do, not to mention real work, if I was going to help anyone at all.

Before Uncle Hendrik drove me home, I sat with Elisabeth a while in her room. She showed me some family pictures she'd managed to salvage from the wreckage of her life in Holland. One of her and Johannes with their arms around a woolly dog. Another of the baby twins snuggled in their mother's lap. And the sweetest of all, Elisabeth, her arms full of irises and her face full of laughter. I had a troublesome lump in my throat. How I wished I could bring that face back to life like that again. Just sweep away all the sadness.

"You are my best friend in the whole world," I said,

wrapping my arms around her for a goodbye hug. "Thank you for letting me help you plant the trees today." I got an extra big hug back.

"Let us always be best friends," she whispered and gave me just a hint of a smile.

Still, there was so much sorrow in those eyes. Could I, or anyone, help erase it? Even the sunny walls of her room and the crisp lace curtains at the windows seemed to have lost their magic.

Uncle Hendrik dropped me off just as Daddy and Uncle Billy were returning from the funeral. Billy let Daddy out in the driveway, so we walked together into the house. I put his coat and hat into the front hall closet while he sank into the nearest chair.

"Are you tired, Daddy?" I asked. Perhaps the day had worn him out, especially considering such sad circumstances.

"World weary, maybe. It's tough saying goodbye to a buddy." Daddy ran his fingers through his hair. "Particularly one so young. Think of it. Murphy survived the war, only to fall victim to some idiot who'd had too many beers. Life can throw you the biggest doggone curve once in a while. And just when you think your life's settled."

"Was it a nice funeral, Daddy?"

"It was short, but dignified. A couple of local guys we knew at Old Farms Convalescent Hospital spoke. Said real nice things about Murphy. Guess he was a real powerhouse for the Blinded Veterans Association." Daddy paused to do a lot of throat clearing. "And that goldarn dog. Billy told me Montgomery stayed right next to the casket during the whole ceremony. All banged up but wouldn't budge the whole time. Can't get that out of my mind."

And that's when I knew what I had to do. Daddy needed to be a part of the world outside our house and his workshop. And I bet there were plenty of fellows just like him. I figured if he could just get out there and meet some of them, maybe the Eddie Howard that Spud first met would come back to life. I'd made a deal with Rory Lee Murphy. He was about to make good on his end, and I knew what I had to do to make good on mine.

The card Mr. Spud had given me was still in my butterfly box. Each time I took it out, hoping I might talk to Daddy and convince him we should call the number the boy private had written there, I made sure to return it to the box for safekeeping.

After a late lunch Daddy and Billy went out to the workshop. I'd already thought out what I planned to do. With my heart thumping a drumroll in my chest, I went out to the hall and dialed the number. In my best imitation of Mama's "I mean business" voice, I finally got through to someone at the VA hospital who gave me just the information I needed. I also left a message and my number. And then it was time to talk to Grandma.

"You did what?" Grandma asked, her voice rising higher in surprise. She was sitting in the living room, an open book in her lap.

"I called the VA hospital. Turns out that the number Mr. Murphy gave me was the office of a lady who helps veterans get connected with guide dogs. We had a really nice talk. But I was particularly interested in Montgomery. Grandma, he would be perfect for Daddy, don't you think?"

"Land sakes, Sweetpea, does your daddy know about any of this?"

Grandma put her book down on the end table and studied my face. "Child, you can't go around arranging your daddy's life. Besides, I'm not sure you can just take over Montgomery. For heaven's sake, there must be rules for this kind of thing."

"Well, turns out Montgomery is with one of the fellows who spoke at the funeral. Another pilot who was at the hospital in Connecticut. I left our number for him to call."

"Now, what's your daddy going to say when he does?"

"I left my name." I stared out the window, biting my lip. "I asked him to call me." And that was when I told Grandma all about the deal I'd made with Mr. Murphy that afternoon and that we'd sealed it with a handshake. And that I certainly intended to make good on my promise.

When the call came, Grandma answered it and handed me the phone. She didn't budge an inch out of the hall but listened to every word. Once I put down the phone, she shook her head and motioned me into her room where she closed the door.

"OK, Sweetpea, it sounded to me like you invited this pilot fellow to drop by after dinner. I'm not sure you've thought all of this out. This family's gone through a lot of changes in the past few years. You have to be ready for a few big new ones. Plus, I can't help but wonder if your mama will be too happy about you rearranging her family's future while she's away at work."

"I know. I always want things to be perfect." I couldn't help but think of how terrified I was when I thought Mama and Mr. Capaldi were having an affair. I was ready to shut Mama out. "The lady I talked to said that getting his own dog would mean Daddy would most likely have to go to California for a while. To the guide dog school. But it wouldn't be for long."

"Well, Annie Leigh, let your old grandma tell you one thing I know for sure. Change is often difficult to deal with, but it is inevitable. Even if we wanted to, we couldn't keep from facing changes in our lives, no matter how much we might want things to stay the same." She reached over and brushed her hand through my hair. "Look at what's happened to you already, and not much of it has been scary. You've met Jon and Elisabeth. Why, the VanderVeldes are almost like family. You've found your artistic side. If our lives never changed, we couldn't grow. We'd all just stay the same."

"I guess that would be kind of boring, huh, Grandma?"

"I guess it would make life very boring, indeed. But why all this rush to get your daddy's life all sorted out now, this minute? I mean, that new baby will mean changes galore."

The answer to Grandma's question was going to take a while, so I went over and crawled up onto her bed. She pulled a chair right up next to me.

"I was pretty little when Daddy went away to war, but I remember a lot about what he was like before. I haven't seen much of that father since he came back. And for a long time now he's separated himself from almost everything except us and the carpentry business. Since we moved here, it's like he's shut himself off even more."

"I suppose you're right. Before he went away to the war, the house was always full of friends. He certainly had a ton of things going on when he was at Whitman College. But blindness does have its limitations."

"That's just it, Grandma. Spud Murphy didn't let his blindness keep him from having a life. I know it sounds strange, but he made me see what Daddy might be able to do. Mr. Murphy didn't let his blindness limit him. He was out there meeting people and doing things. He even let me see my old Daddy for a few minutes. That afternoon when I walked Spud to the car and made him a promise, I knew it was one I had to keep."

"That's my girl. There's that Annie Leigh Howard feistiness I know and love so well. How can I help?"

"Well, for starters, you can help me when Mr. Gavin Rooney gets here. We have to make sure that Mama is on our side and doesn't get all starchy and that Daddy doesn't go all standoffish on us."

"Gavin Rooney. Land sakes, child, another Irishman. That hospital must have had a whole platoon. I'll talk to your mama. As for your daddy — well, you're on your own."

"Just promise me one thing, Grandma."

"What's that, sweetie?"

"Don't you ever change."

Grandma started to laugh. "I'll try my best, but you have to promise me something."

"What's that?"

"Try not to grow up too fast. I miss that little girl who made hollyhock dolls with Gloria out by the creek. I need a bit more time to get used to this new young lady who I expect is going to help all of us find our best selves."

"It's a deal, Grandma." And we sealed our bargain by going straight to the kitchen and making ourselves triple scoop banana splits with extra sprinkles.

Chapter 27

Easter morning I woke up to the sound of tapping on my bedroom door. It was Grandma, her hair a big cloud all round her head like an enormous dandelion puff.

"My land, Sweetpea, get a move on. The whole house has overslept." She was cradling her best crepe dress in her arms like a baby. "We're going to be late for church. And wouldn't you know it, this needs to be pressed, and what's more, we have rain for Easter Sunday and my new hat will be absolutely ruined." She scurried off down the hall, making little mouse squeaks of distress.

I dashed into the cold bathroom, brushed my teeth, splashed a little water on my face, and hurried back to my room to get dressed. Mama had already laid out a new dress, navy blue with the sailor collar, the very one I'd seen at Rhodes department store. Every Easter morning since the year I was three, I'd found a spanking new outfit and a basket full of chocolate eggs and a surprise gift waiting for me when I woke up. I loved to get the dresses, and the surprise was always something really special. I'd been such a goof, I wasn't sure I deserved something special this year. But there, on the top of my dresser, was a small box with several tubes of watercolors and three brushes tied together with a pink bow. Mama understood me after all.

Before going into the kitchen I knocked softly on Mama and Daddy's bedroom door. Daddy opened it a smidge. "I'm staying home with your mama. She's dead tired, and the fresh paint in the kitchen is making her feel queasy."

They'd both stayed up for hours talking to Gavin Rooney and his wife, who'd arrived promptly at eight o'clock with Montgomery and apparently stayed until near midnight. I'd pretended to read at the dining room table, listening in, but had finally given up at eleven and gone to bed.

Daddy and Mama had surprised me by agreeing to take Spud's dog, once they found out he needed a home. I figured Daddy overruled Mama on that one. Uncle Billy had taken Montgomery up to the garage apartment for the night.

Out in the kitchen, Uncle Billy was rushing around trying to figure out how to make coffee and iron a shirt at the same time. He knew better than to ask Grandma to iron it for him. "Give me a hand, will you, kid? I promised to pick up Lydia on my way to the service."

I took over the ironing, certain Billy would burn a hole in

the collar before he'd barely started.

"How's Montgomery?" I asked, trying to iron out the wrinkles that my uncle had ironed in.

"He was good as gold. Hope he helps your dad get used to having a dog around. Get him to thinking about one of his own."

"I was hoping Montgomery would be Daddy's guide dog," I said, holding out the shirt.

"I asked Gavin about that. Doesn't work that way. Your dad will train with his own dog." Uncle Billy handed me his cup of coffee and struggled into his shirt. "Lydia and I'll meet you and Ma at the church." He took back his coffee, gulped a couple of swallows, plunked his cup in the sink and was out the door, pulling on his jacket. I hoped he looked in his rearview mirror before he got to Lydia's. His hair looked like he'd just gotten out of bed. Which, of course, he had. Rushing off to First Baptist, even on Easter, was not my uncle's usual Sunday routine.

Grandma wasn't one bit fooled, taking in the dirty cup in the sink and the burned toast on the drain board. "Already off to church, is he?" she said with a chuckle. "I'd like to think it's his newfound faith, but I doubt it's his soul your uncle's trying to save."

Just as the two of us left the house, the sky cleared and the sun even peeped out a bit. Grandma's new straw hat was safe for the moment.

All the way to church Grandma made a fuss over the millions of daffodils bursting with color in every front yard. "And look at those early pink rhoddies," she said, driving into the church parking lot. "Even a bit soggy they're lovely."

Uncle Billy and Miss Moore had saved us seats, and we squeezed ourselves into the pew. I could hardly concentrate on the service for all their exchanges of dopey looks and cow eyes. It was pretty nauseating.

By the time we got back home, the smell of baking ham filled every room. Grandma took off her hat, the ribbon a bit wilted from the damp, threw on an apron, and started in on her ambrosia salad, almost as famous in Walla Walla as her Fourth of July potato salad. She was proudest of her secret ingredient, the pineapple dressing.

I found Daddy out in the backyard with Montgomery. "I've been walking him in circles around the house, but now that you're home we can take him on a proper walk." He handed me the leash. "I think Ella Mae is going to have shin splints. I swear I could hear her dashing back and forth in her yard ever since I brought Montgomery out."

"She's gone into the house now, Daddy, but her curtains are twitching."

"Be prepared. She and the mister are invited to dinner. Your mama and I felt it was the right thing to do."

"Where should we walk, Daddy?"

"Just around the neighborhood," he said. "But let's make it a long one. "

"Mama won't be happy if I stay away too long."

"Don't worry, your grandma will have everything under control. And believe me, your Uncle Billy will be in there trying to outdo everyone to impress his Miss Moore. I set the dishes out buffet style while you were all at church."

We'd have a full house later. The VanderVeldes were coming, of course. Tante Dee had to get an Easter meal for the main house first. Belle and ol' Larry were coming, and now the Hinkles. Daddy and I needed to have some time alone while we could. We had a lot to talk over, and I'd been hoping we'd find time to do just that.

After we'd walked in silence for a bit, I decided to jump right in. "So what did Mr. Rooney have to say?"

"I've been thinking a lot about our conversation. What really impressed me was hearing about some of my buddies from Old Farms." Daddy reached over for my free arm. "I mean, some of those guys have gone back to college. They're even teaching school."

"Would you like to go back to college, Daddy?"

"If things had turned out differently, I probably would have gone back to school, what with the G.I. Bill and everything. As things turned out, I never even considered it. And I wasn't about to back out on my deal with Billy to start our own carpentry business."

"You could still do it — go back to school that is, if you wanted to." I thought I heard something different in Daddy's voice, maybe a hint that he figured he just might do more than he'd ever thought possible.

"I'm not sure I could manage that now. You know what they say about old dogs and new tricks." He stopped and leaned over to give Montgomery a pat. "Nothing personal, old fellow."

"Don't you sometimes just want to get out and see what you can do, like Spud Murphy? Seemed like he was traveling and doing all kinds of things."

"Well, my girl," said Daddy, "I suppose you think I've taken the easy way, stuck close to home, too cautious about how I'd fare in the outside world." Daddy stopped and rubbed his chin for a second. "I mean, I've hardly ventured out using my cane. And honestly, I'd have to admit you'd be right about that."

We were close to the bus bench, so I steered us over there, and we sat down. Montgomery lay down right next to us.

"Spud's death made me realize how quickly our lives can change — in an instant. Any day could be your last, you know. But doing the kind of things Spud was doing would take me away from home from time to time. I missed so much of your early years, I don't want to miss out on any more. And with the new baby coming, we'll have our hands full."

"But think what you could be doing! And besides, Mama

will have lots of help. Gilly's been at the shop long enough to help manage it for the next few months. And you know Grandma won't be able to stay away for long. I promise to be better about doing my chores." I suppose it was silly of me to stew over my promise to Spud, but I kept thinking how excited he was about recruiting Daddy. "Mr. Rooney asked you to take Mr. Murphy's place, didn't he?"

Daddy didn't answer right away. "What's that wonderful smell? My guess is it's wisteria. I can see some purple blob over yonder."

"Yes, it's wisteria. It's growing on the wall next to Wolfe's Market. C'mon, Daddy. What did you say to Mr. Rooney?"

"Yes, he did ask me to step in and take over for Spud, as a kind of regional advisor. I said I'd think about it." Daddy held his hand up to feel the wind. "I sniff rain in the air. I believe we're going to get another shower. Best be on our way."

We walked in silence for a bit, Daddy holding the leash while Montgomery padded alongside. I put my arm through Daddy's and gave his a squeeze. "You know you'd be perfect. Why, you can talk to all kinds of folks. And I bet you'd get to travel a bit."

"You trying to get me out of the house?" Daddy reached over and mussed my hair. "Hmmm! Is there something you aren't telling me?"

"Don't be silly."

"If I did that I'd have to be away, maybe for long stretches. That would leave your mama in a fix. What about your Uncle Billy? He'd be on his own a lot. Come to think of it, I'd most likely have to brush up on my Braille. I haven't used it much since the hospital."

"I think you should do it, Daddy. You could get your own dog. I have the number to call. Mr. Murphy gave it to me."

"I'm still not convinced you aren't just trying to get me out of your hair." Daddy stopped just long enough to give me a big hug. "I'll talk to Gavin, and I won't make any decisions without consulting you. You have to keep in mind that would mean some more major changes and everything won't be settled all at once."

"Grandma says we can't grow without change, and I know she's right. You have to promise to think about all this, Daddy." We'd reached the front steps, so I stopped to help Daddy up the stairs. "Seriously, please think about it."

"Whoa there, my girl. I promise, truly. Any other 'serious' stuff you need to talk about?"

Lately, I'd noticed the gentle way Mama looked at Daddy, and the way they'd begun to laugh out loud at jokes no one else seemed to hear. "Are you and Mama OK?"

"Come here, you." Daddy held out his arms, and I slipped right into them, getting tangled in Montgomery's leash at the same time. "Is that what's been worrying you all this time?"

"Sort of."

"Well, don't worry your head about us. Your mama and I, we're doing fine. Can't say I'm completely on board with her working so hard. But your mama has a mind of her own, as you well know, and Lord knows I wouldn't want a clinging vine. So no, we aren't ideal, but everything's going to be all right. I can promise you that." He gave me a knuckle tap on my head. "What other stuff you got wedged in that noggin of yours?"

"I'm worried about Elisabeth. The war . . . it was so awful for her."

"I know, honey, your grandma's told me some of it. But you're being a good friend, and that's important. Dee and Hendrik are real glad you got Elisabeth back to her drawing. Guess it's really helped pull her round." I felt Daddy's arms tighten around me again. "And that boy. He's sure sweet on you. You've helped him through some rough spots. I have that on good authority. Just continue to be yourself."

Before we could say any more, the grand Lincoln had pulled up in front. As usual, everyone got out of the car carrying a plate or a tray of something Tante Dee had baked.

Elisabeth had on a new black skirt, one of the ballerina length ones that were all the rage. She was carrying a chocolate cake, at least six layers. Daddy had barely stepped into the hall when Uncle Hendrik cornered him, full of questions about the Russians, and they walked together into the house complaining bitterly about the Communists. The radio had been full of news all week about the U.S. plane shot down over the Baltic Sea. I'd barely said hi to Elisabeth when Johannes grabbed my hand, and we went over to sit on the porch swing.

"I have something for you," he whispered into my ear.

I studied the silver box in his hand, wondering what in the world he'd brought me and what I would do if I didn't like it. I was still thinking about my conversation with Daddy and couldn't help but wonder just who I was when I was "just myself."

I looked at Johannes and saw he was holding a heart-shaped gold locket. Without thinking, I turned so he could clasp the chain around my neck. I closed my eyes for a moment and held the heart against my throat, tracing the lacy pattern etched on the surface. A calm settled over me that felt right, natural. When I opened my eyes, he was bending over to kiss me, a quick, light kiss on the cheek.

"Annie," he said, "you have given me so much. I give you my heart."

Hand in hand we went into the house, where everyone was gathered around the dining table, admiring the ham. Elisabeth had not wanted to leave Montgomery alone and had stayed in the living room with him stretched out near her feet. She was scratching his ears and singing softly just for him. Ella Mae had taken her usual two plates, but I noticed she hesitated before putting one back. Progress? Maybe. Mama had been complaining about the paint smell, and just before she'd left the room to throw up, Daddy had been joking around, reminding her she not only got a freshly painted kitchen but also a new electric stove in the bargain. Uncle Billy had been looking kind of sheepish all day, and I wondered if he and Miss Moore had had their first lover's quarrel. She was chatting happily with Belle, who'd arrived by taxi, ol' Larry having been delayed by a last-minute emergency flower delivery to the country club.

About the time we began to fill our plates, the rain started again, a real April shower. I hoped it wasn't spoiling too many egg hunts. Not a perfect Easter, but I knew I could handle it. Whatever happened in the future, I hoped I could handle that, too. Some things were a given. Mama certainly wasn't done bossing everyone around, and Uncle Billy was still working some things out. Daddy, Elisabeth, and Johannes had more healing to do before their world would seem safe again. And no one seemed to know what the Russians were going to do. Plus, folks were saying Korea was the next thing to worry about. But on that Easter Sunday afternoon, surrounded by everyone I cared about most, I could settle for less than perfect.

Acknowledgments

I would like to thank the many good friends who helped make this book possible. I am especially indebted to my writing group: Gina Capaldi, Leah Key, Q.L. Pearce, Andra Simmons, and Fran Rusackas. I also owe thanks to LeAnn Miller who read an early draft and offered such wise advice. A special thank you to Mae Key Ketter who gave me the valuable perspective that only an eleven-year-old could offer. Thanks go to Carmen Fought, who has never stopped cheering me on from the sidelines. Betty Kovacs, my dearest friend, gets a special mention for her continued support and encouragement.

Grateful appreciation to Walter Werkhoven, VIST Coordinator at the VA Puget Sound Health Care System, Tacoma, WA, for answering my many questions about the experiences of a WWII blinded soldier and so graciously outlining the history of resources for blinded veterans. He also gave generously of his time by reading an early draft and sharing his responses. Enormous thanks also go to Stuart Nelson, Manager of Communications for the Blinded Veterans Association. His continuing support, advice, and general helpfulness have been extraordinary. Thanks also go to Lorri Bernson, Media and Community Liaison at Guide Dogs of America, Sylmar, CA. Any errors are mine alone.

I would like to thank Faye Bloom of the Tacoma Public Library as well as Jody Gripp and Brian Kamens from the Northwest Room. I am in their debt.

I am grateful to Jon Prins for helping me understand the experience of children in wartime by sharing parts of his young life in the Netherlands.

Special appreciation to Eerdmans and Kathleen Merz and, most particularly, my editor Jeanne Elders DeWaard, whose excellent critiques were consistently thoughtful and perceptive. Most of all I must thank my husband Jack, always my invaluable first reader. And our children, Christopher, Gregory, and Kevin.